Memoirs from A Parallel Universe™
Universe 2285 X 10^∞

Jake
and the
Treasure
of
Solomon Lake

Lawrence BoarerPitchford

DEDICATION

Dedicated to family and friends who never gave up on my
dream to entertain.

DISCLAIMER

The story and events are purely the construct of the
author. Any relation to persons living or dead are purely
coincidental.

CONTENTS

Acknowledgments   i

1   A Baleful Start   Pg #2

2   Destiny is a Best Practice   Pg #15

3   Nowhere Like Home   Pg #23

4   Best Laid Plans of Aliens and Men   Pg #31

5   No Other   Pg #39

6   Where Fools Dare   Pg #46

7   Flight of the Silver Horn   Pg #54

8   The Gentler Gamester   Pg #60

9   A Stich In Time   Pg #67

10   The Flea in the Ointment   Pg #75

ACKNOWLEDGMENTS

Senior Editor ~ Wendy Schirmer

Copy Editor ~ Roselyn Pitchford

Cover Art ~ Boarerpitchford.com

CHAPTER 1
A Baleful Start

It wasn't the stench of urine that made Jake hate Detention 3 Ward. It wasn't the dozen bone-bags that wandered the D3, growling and showing contempt that made him hate where he was. And, it definitely wasn't the terrible tasting clotted chope-reed sap that he had to eat that made him hate the D3. It was the fact that the charges that put him in the D3 were bullshit.

They were bullshit because he'd not been near the Valencia hanger when the half dozen city law-bots were destroyed. Jake didn't beat the six law-officers and leave them for dead. And, those three fly-cars that were smashed and dismembered, Jake absolutely didn't do that. No, it was very safe to say that Jake wasn't anywhere near that commotion; he was ten miles away committing a murder. Well, at least a murder in the eyes of the law.

"Facebreaker! Come to the portal and await further instructions," a voice commanded over the intercom. Jake stood up and walked the fifteen feet to the glowing hole in the wall and waited. "Insert your hands and wait for the click." He did so. A tight feeling around his wrists made any movement of his hands impossible. The hole opened, and he was pulled through.

Two Valencia City law-men in armor stood in front of him. One lifted his visor and looked Jake in the eye. "I was sure it was you, Jake, but your visa chip showed you were at the Sulking Lounge downtown all night, and though there's no imagery to show it. The chip don't lie."

Jake shrugged. "I guess even an educated and well-groomed fellow such as you can make mistakes." He took the box that contained his gear from the property clerk and turned to follow the line pulsating a yellowish hue to freedom. With curious eyes, he looked up at the large law-man. "So, Bob, that smell on your breath isn't wayfare quif is it?"

Bob lurched for Jake – his hands balled into fists. "I'll rip your melon from its perch," he shouted but was blocked by his partner.

"Hold up, Bob…don't let em get to ya! He's just a stroid-joker, just a bummer," the other officer said.

Jake smiled, turned, and followed the yellow line to a door. As he exited, the cuffs sluffed off and fell into the room behind him. He was now unhindered and free to get back to the business of living.

He came down to the first floor, then out onto the streets of Valencia. "Great," Jake muttered, "Nogging rain… of course it would be rain…"

Rain fell in torrents as Jake walked down Hills Avenue. The tilted and neglected buildings of the Gim'etal quarter looked like ruins from a lost civilization. One structure, ten stories high, was missing a wall, and all the floors were visible, some with rotted and broken furniture. Another building had holes, the size of pie pans, probably from the insurrection of 3014. He turned down Whisker Street and passed by the Tiberius Columns of the Yate's Hotel. A single neon sign flickered on and off, casting twisted shadows and a dark red light along the coal-black street.

Jake stepped under the awning of the hotel and pulled from his wet shirt pocket a zip-stick and put the feed into his mouth. Triggering the element, he drew in the musky vapor and felt his lungs open up. His thoughts cleared. His blood pumped through his body, and the thump-thump in his ears was nearly deafening. Taking a second hit, he looked up into the darkness of the stormy night and knew he needed to get back up there, back into the ink. It was the only place he felt in control. Now, all he had to do was collect the second payment for his skullduggery... get the final repairs done to his ship...cast adrift from Port Valencia, and head for Heaven's Gate.

"Jake, come on in and take some rasha un-un," a Greto said while stepping out of the hotel's main gate and pretending to light a smoke.

"Rasha un-un..." Jake repeated in a whisper. Unbridled pleasure at the hands of a non-living thing. He looked at it; female - human enough upon inspection, but under that gossamer web of material, just another poorly maintained sex bot. He'd partook as a younger man, doing things that could only be described by the conservative citizen as depraved; after all, they were just machines. But now, he wasn't very sure that there was much distinction between sentient and mach-sentient – life was everywhere, and perhaps everything.

It was the way that Dos Kaparcon had expressed in her thesis,'The Rod of Plank; A Treatise on Existence'. The gist of the document – all five hundred pages – was that even the most elementary state of reality is life, and that means causing death was immoral. Ergo, all things then were alive and required respect for that life. Jake shook his head. Not tonight, ole-boy – way too heavy, he thought.

"Come in for some fun?" The Greto asked as it licked its lips. "I see your cred stock is green – and I'm very cost affordable."

"I've got business to attend to. Maybe another time." Jake took another few puffs from his zip-stick and put it back into his pocket. Stepping out from under the awning, he moved headlong into the wind and driving rain – swaddled nicely into the darkness of the streets.

He crossed Ninety-Second Street and Pine to the pill terminal. Down the steps he went, descending into the poorly lit under-ways of the vacuum pods – affectionately called the pill-box.

Jake's boots clacked as he walked across the metallic platform. A pill was sitting – waiting to be of service. He approached, and it opened a door.

"Where too?" asked a soft feminine voice.

"Wabash and Templeton – cred me," Jake said.

"Your account is green – you are approved," replied the pod.

Jake took the seat facing his destination. The door sealed, and the inside became aglow with the visage of a squire's coach and a country road.

The four-wheeled horse-drawn covered coach swayed slightly. Jake heard no modern sounds, only the gentle blowing breeze just beyond the open carriage window and the clop of a horse's hooves somewhere up ahead.

The sweet smell of pine and wet grass drifted to Jake's nose. An unconscious smile came to his mouth as he thought of the carriage rides he'd taken on Paladin as a livery footman. He was lucky to be rented out as a footman – for many of his friends were rented out as vechy-toys, sex playthings for the rich and powerful.

All Jake had to do was ride a carriage, serve the occupant with drink and food while in transit, and make sure their ride was good and their exit uneventful. He thought of those unlucky friends, many of whom committed suicide.

The planet Paladin was rural agrarian but extremely hedonistic. The Vechymorian religion that dominated the world did not have many taboos, but using birth control was one of them. And, being caught equipped with birth control while on Paladin could lead to one's execution. And it is of note that there were few executions.

Unregulated sex produced millions of unwanted children, and the poor reservations or po-re's were filled to the brim. So, Jake was born into a po-re and reared, with tax donations, into a footman. It was a job he was thankful for – and hated at the same time.

Then, one day a visiting pilot actually spoke to him. "You should break from this chavy-chav and get up there," the pilot pointed at the sky. "There, you can be whatever you want. Make a fortune, and adventure to worlds unexplored!"

Jake looked upward. The sky was dark blue at the top. That word 'fortune' was alien to him –his labors on Paladin served to provide room and board only. But there was something else – something up there to get to.

A year later, he escaped the po-re, made his way to the largest town on the coast, and stowed away on a steamship to the largest city on the planet. Once there, he stole and committed violence, all to get into the spaceport. It took a few days to figure out how to get inside the facility and onto a ship – but once he did, Jake resolved never to return to Paladin.

Once off-world and among the stars, he remade himself – becoming Jake 'Facebreaker' Sharkar – later just known as Jake Facebreaker. Dark things he did to survive all those years, to build a reputation of a bummer who could get things done – in places where doing such shenanigans could get one killed.

It was interesting how the quantronics of the pill and its connected systems always knew what he was thinking – deep down. He never remembered to ask to have the effect shut off (maybe he secretly didn't want it turned off). So, he often suffered those fragments from his memories, things he'd thought he had shut out. Those images from deep within him appeared on the walls of the pill intending to make his ride pleasant, but often doing the exact opposite.

Jake felt the subtle effects of the transport decelerating. A red light flashed, and the image surrounding him faded to the stark white of the inside of the pill. The door opened, and he stepped out onto the platform at Templeton.

He took the numo-tube up to the ground level and found the hurry-along that led to the Price Turner Building. There, he was allowed access and was led up to the ten thousand block – where an automodroid let him into a sally port door.

"Jake?" The voice was obfuscated. "You will be scanned. Standby."

An intense light flashed, Jake's artificial retinas went dark. A moment later a door opened, and he was shoved forcibly into an expansive loft partially covered with white shag carpet.

A dark-skinned man wearing a bright red robe of synth-silk approached and handed Jake an orb of whisky. "Take this, go sit on the sofa and indulge in a huff from the new hookah I printed this morning."

"Michael," Jake acknowledged with a nod as he sat and took a draw from the hookah stem. The blast was powerful – most likely plenty-rosebud, a powerful drug in high favor with the elites of the city. For a moment, Jake lived several lifetimes – all in his dreamy head. Upon his last death, his eyes cleared, and his hand reflexively brought up the orb. He drank down the last of the whisky.

"Fuck…" was all Jake said.

"Good – right?" Michael asked.

Jake nodded – still not sure if he was just living another drug-induced life.

"The after-effect – the disorientation will wear off soon. Nonetheless, here's your payment for a job well done." Michael set a box down on the table in front of Jake and opened the lid.

The top vanished, and inside was a navkey. Jake blinked a few times and shook his head. "What the hell is this?"

"It's a navkey," Michael said with a grin that showed off his backlit-teeth implants. He sat next to Jake and put his hand on Jake's leg. "It's my gift to you for being such a good sport."

Jake looked sideways at Michael, who removed his hand and sat back a bit.

"No offense intended," Michael added.

"We agreed on cred, not this," Jake said – his voice remaining even – vacant of threat or acceptance.

Michael smiled and shook his head. "Listen, blister, your work speaks for itself. You helped me out of a serious spot. The cred we agreed upon is not worthy of a fellow like you. So, I figured you might want something a bit more valuable. This navkey leads to a location that will set you up for life - and is untraceable to me – of course." He crossed his legs and his robe opened a bit, exposing his nude body under.

"Leads to what?" Jake asked, his wits coming back to him.

"You're familiar with the legend of Solomon Lake?" Michael asked.

"A little. I've heard some things around." Jake looked down at the navkey. "You're telling me that there lie the coordinates to the Solomon Lake treasure?"

Michael nodded. "Yup." His voice was filled with giddy excitement.

"Nope – not good. Just give me the cred," Jake told him.

"The balance of your payment is in an escrow, as agreed. But, instead of money as a reward... if you're willing to help me out, you and I can be very rich – and not planet rich either – I mean galaxy rich," Michael said.

"Galaxy rich?" Jake's interest piqued. "How so?"

The expression on Michael's face was one of incomprehensible disbelief. "The treasure, from the looting of the Chilean ruins on Old Camp Fodder. It's said what Lake found was worth the combined wealth of all the Host systems."

Jake sat quietly. He looked down at the navkey, then back up at Michael. "We'll go halves on the return?"

"Sure, anything you say. Or, you could take the cred – and I'll find another Dilbert to help me… but I'm offering you a chance to make an off-the-rack fortune. Set for life – if you don't mind me saying."

Michael took up one of the octopus arms of the hookah, took a long draw, and sat back. Drool dripped down the corner of his mouth, as he mumbled and moaned – spired in some pleasure undreamt.

Jake picked up the navkey and glanced over to his ebony patron. Getting up, he filled his orb with more whisky, and sat opposite Michael and the box. Drinking down the contents in one draft, he thought for some time if it was worth the coal-raking he'd be taking if he said yes.

Michael twitched and mumbled – a bubble of drool forming over his lips. Jake went for more whisky.

"Did… did you say you'd do it?" Michael finally asked as he wiped the slobber from his mouth with the corner of his robe. He sat forward and, with a shaking hand, reached for his orb.

Jake looked down at the navkey again – licked his lips, then said, "I'm not without concerns, but I'm your man."

"You lively donker!" Michael laughed. "You – me – and all the cutter we can ferret!"

"Okay – you're putting up the money to have my ship repaired. Then – it's into the dark and straight for that explorer-zed," Jake said.

"Not quite," Michael stated. "We'll need to make a stop first. We need to make way to Kyper's Pass Port. Just because I know where the goods are, doesn't mean I know how to get the goods."

"Okay – send eight thousand creds to Mulper Astro-mechanics, and they'll do the last bit of fixing. Then, we can head up," Jake told Michael.

"Already done!" Michael said, then laughed loudly before putting the bulb down and dancing about the room like an Irish lunatic.

"Jake Shakar – you have been gone two days. You are in arrears for twenty-four hours. May I charge your account?" asked the hotel automaster as Jake entered the front door.

"Call me Jake Facebreaker," Jake said.

"But, that is not your legal visa name," said the automaster

"Charge me, I got the creds," Jake said.

The display in his ocular-visor showed a debit.

"Charged and approved," the automaster said. "Room access is now available."

Jake nodded and headed for the vertical relay. He waited, and the door opened. Stepping into his room, he felt it move as it was deposited back into the structure of the hotel.

"There is a message for you, sir," the automaster said over the comm.

"Sure, lay it on me," Jake said.

The voice was distorted. "Mr. Facebreaker – as per your request, your ship's last repairs will be finalized in three days," spoke the voice.

"The quantum tracking number was scrambled," said the automaster. "Is that a standard business practice?"

"You know it isn't," Jake replied. "Now, connect me to the reach-out service.

"Will this be on the record, or off the record?" the automaster asked.

"Okay – fine. It's off the record, and it's only fair that I compensate you," Jake stated and saw his debit amount go up in his ocular-visor.

"For any inconvenience, such as law enforcement asking questions," the automaster said. "I can claim a programming error from time to time – for my more discerning clients."

"That's why I keep coming here," Jake replied.

"Another message coming in for you," the automaster said.

"Encrypted, or no?" Jake asked.

"Encrypted," replied the automaster.

I'll take it in my ear," Jake said. He directed his thoughts to the inner ear comm. It came on.

"Jake – it's you know who. I have some news. My contact moved from Kyper's Pass Port and is now residing as a magistrate on Paladin. We'll need to head to Paladin when we leave orbit. Let me know when the ship is ready." The comm faded out.

"Paladin..?" Jake said with a thick tone of dismay. "Son-of-a-bitch!"

Jake sat on the bed and took off his boots and put his feet up. "Paladin?" he said again. "Of all the planets in all the Host Systems – why in hell did he move to Paladin?"

Shaking his head, Jake took in a deep breath, held it, then exhaled. "Oh well – the great universal programmer has one hell of a sense of humor," he said aloud.

Closing his eyes, he envisioned the entertainment service and it became active in his view. Sixty-five thousand channels, and only a thousand had anything of any real interest on them.

"Silent room," Jake said – a common phrase that secured a room from listening devices and the hotel management systems. He thought of the quantum channel for the reach-out service Interlink, and he was connected. "Show me all the information on Solomon Lake and his treasure."

A series of holographic columns appeared with small images along all three axes. Jake scrolled through them, then found one that read, 'Alternate-reality assumptions of Solomon Lake's treasure'. He activated it.

In an instant, Jake was over the shoulder of an artificially intelligent character that looked exactly like the once-living Solomon Lake. There was a narration option, and Jake switched it on.

"Solomon Lake, a former prospector, miner, Host System's marshal and governor, was looking to test out a new process for distance elimination travel when he selected a coordinate that took him to an uncharted solar system. There he scanned a planet that would later be called Old Camp Fodder."

Jake followed Solomon around as he set the travel vectors into an old finger-driven interface. The viewing ports went black, the ship shook, and then the ship was in orbit around a blue-colored planet with a distant orange star.

"After running surface scans – he discovered non-natural anomalies littering the globe. In his excitement, he tripped down to the surface. There, he discovered the ruins of a once vibrant and advanced civilization."

Solomon took a drop-ship, went down, and stepped out onto a concourse surrounded by decaying ruins of mighty structures that once dominated the landscape. He set up an antenna and presses some buttons on it.

"Laying claim to the planet, Solomon Lake began to explore. And, it was there in the very first alien ruins that he discovered The Treasure," said the voiceover.

The cache of alien items was clearly props made to look like what humans thought the Solomon Lake alien technology should look like - exotic, organic things, pulsing with light, surrounded by glowing hovering orbs, and giving off odd sounds with occasional beeps.

Ten minutes followed as Solomon commanded construction and prospector bots to load the vast items into his ship. Once all was looted, he turned back to Jake and winked.

"That's it. Now to hide this treasure so no one will steal it from me," Solomon said. He boarded his ship, and from a position on the ground, Jake watched it rise and zoom off into the atmosphere.

A small disclaimer flashed in Jake's eye, followed by a request for financial support for the producer. Jake's implants cleared, and he was again looking at the interior of his rented room.

"Jake, the police are here. Something about a murder…" the automaster proclaimed. "Do you wish to see them, or should I unlock the utility access to the inner infrastructure of this building?"

"Option number two," Jake said while grabbing his utility belt, shoes, and dock-side gear.

He made for the back of the room. A small hatch clicked, and he opened it. There he saw a connecting accessway to the inner workings that managed the rooms within the building. Once through, the door clicked again. He tried it – it was locked.

The building began to move. A loud mechanical hum followed, and the large boxes that made up the rooms were shifting. Another habitat came close, and Jake jumped to that room's alcove.

His feet slid, and he found himself prone on the platform. He quickly put on his boots. The whirling of large boxes flew past and swung around. Jake saw another alcove – he jumped – and fell prone again.

The movement stopped. He crawled out onto the side of one room. Above him was the skylight. He got to the top of the box. The whirling sound echoed – he jumped and grabbed onto a pipe just below the glass windows. The room fell away and was replaced by another.

Jake thought it was lucky that there were Inertial-dampeners that kept the occupants happily ignorant of the shifting rooms. Without them, it would be impossible to enjoy their stay.

"Jake – I'm on a secure channel," the automaster said.

"They're making it decidedly difficult to lie to them. If they call a prog-hammer, they'll know that I opened the hatch for you."

"A little busy here," Jake thought to the automaster.

"Ah – I suppose you would be. I see you're hanging on for dear life. Here," the automaster said.

The skylight seal popped. Some air was released. Jake lifted his body mass up, then slung his right hand onto the metal window edge. He hooked his leg onto the pipe, then got his boot on it.

"I owe you one!" Jake said aloud, as he slithered through the skylight and rolled onto the tar-pebble rooftop.

"Come again. I mean when you're not in such high demand by public servants," the automaster replied.

Chapter 2
Destiny is a Best Practice

Jake moved toward the center of the roof. Most likely, the enforcement squad hadn't shifted any remote sensing solutions to this location yet. He called up a flycar and hunkered down by the fusion power plant and cooling system. The taxi appeared and flew just over the lip of the building.

Moving to the car, Jake jumped in - approving the cred debit at the same time. The car took off. He was heading for the old part of the city – one of the many suburra that littered the planet, just like on all the densely populated planets. No Valencia cop would set foot in there without a backup military escort and air support. It was the beating heart of the underworld that lived behind those stalwart black walls that enclosed the Legacy Sector.

The flycar swooped in and deposited Jake on a dilapidated rooftop. No sooner did Jake's boots hit the tarpaper and metal roof, the car then made for safer pastures.

Jake went for the roof access door. He flung it open and headed into the darkness of the stairwell. There was a strange smell – that of someone cooking synth-meat with off-world spices. As he hit the top floor, he saw the walls of the various rooms. They were demolished by knuckle-thumpers using sledgehammers looking to ward off built-up anxieties due to poverty. He moved downward.

At the bottom of the building, Jake waited at the glass door that opened onto the boulevard. Crowds of people moved just beyond the frosted window. The Legacy Sector was impacted by migrant souls seeking a better life. Unfortunately, they would not find it in Valencia.

Jake pushed open the door and stepped out into the flow of pedestrian traffic. Down the street he went, avoiding the gaze of the occasional pillager, and making sure his organs were protected.

He came to a Java-Haus and went inside. His interlink connected and was able to lock onto the comm network. Crafting a message, Jake used his Q-encrypt setting. The message was away, and zooming from satellite to ground station, to wireless, to laser-com.

Jake got a cup of coffee, or 'black-sauce' as the pilot-slang went. He slipped outside and down the street to a Hudo-Flat, where he secured a room for the night. Looking at his planet-time indicator, star-set was coming, and he didn't want to get killed wandering the tippy-shacks of the Legacy in the dark. He'd hold up for the night in the small sleeper, then at dawn find a pill box, and head to the repair hangers to stay on his ship until Michael arrived.

Jake crawled into the one-person sleeper chamber and sealed the hatch. 'No frills and no thrills' the small black on white sign read at the far end. The habitat was just big enough and high enough for a person to lay flat, and if necessary, sit up and turn around if needed. A small ledge held a cup and a water dispenser, and at the far end, was a pillow wrapped in a case of blue bacteria-killing synth-cloth.

He found the vend-slot near the front of the chamber and ordered a meal – two sandwiches and a can of Hardball lemon-flavored vodka. Out of the slot popped his items.

He ate and drank, then sat back and called forth a novel from his list of books – ten thousand and counting. The cover page opened, The Darklight Affair, a story about the passionate love tryst of a woman star ship captain and her estranged Libervox alien navigator.

Jake read for an hour or so, then turned off the white light, and fell asleep in the soft watery glow of the nightlight. His dreams were complex, and as they stretched on becoming nightmares – he thrashed from side to side, wrapped in the syth-cloth of the bed.

Jake's eyes came open. There was a ping sound in his ear. His alarm had woken him, and he was feeling a staggering sense of exhaustion. "Come on," he whispered. He rolled over and took a hit from his zip-stick.

In his ocular-visor, he saw all the usable communication links. There was a note from Michael.

"Open," Jake said. The written text appeared.

"So, they came seeking you too," Jake said aloud, then chuckled. "Those law-dogs sure are good at what they do."

He sat up, then ordered a snack and a can of self-heating black-sauce. When he was done, he gathered up his stuff and checked out.

Once on the street, he made for the nearest pill-box. There, he got a ride to the spaceport and the repair hangers.

As he hit the fix-it floor of the Mulper Astro-mechanics shop, the bright lights of the hanger blinded him for a second. Millicent Dowdy was at the far end – dressed in an orange jumpsuit and sturdy work boots. She ran the place – beautiful as a sunrise, hard as steel, cold as snow, and utterly corrupt. Jake loved her.

She spotted him from across the hanger floor, waved, then approached. Jake waited.

"Jake – what's the rumpus?" she asked.

"No rumpus. I just wanted to see my favorite ship engineer," Jake said.

She came close, leaned in, and sniffed around his collar and neck. "You stink of the D," she told him.

"How the fuck did you know that?"

She laughed. "You really are a thumper, aren't you," she said. "A friend at Q-Check said she saw the law-bots bring you in. No magic, little Jake – just a woman's superior network."

"I'm a bit pressed. How soon can I bring the engines online and nose up?" Jake asked.

"In a few hours. We still need to make sure the repairs are sound with a test flight," Millicent replied.

"What if I didn't have a few hours?"

"You bastard! You didn't bring the law-bots here, did you?"

"No – of course not. But, it's something you may want to be prepared for," Jake said.

She frowned. "I'm always ready for that call," Millicent replied. "You can have the ship in half an hour if you're going to take her without a test flight. But, if shit goes bust'o – you'd better sing your sob-song on the other side of the galaxy. You get me?" She poked him in the chest twice.

Jake nodded. Above all else, he did not want to ruin his relationship with Millicent. She had a long reach to many systems, and her friends and colleagues would pass news of such a mistake around without delay. Jake wouldn't be able to get a red-wagon fixed anywhere in the Host Systems or beyond.

"No baby – I'd never sing about your work being bad." He fostered a slow smile.

"Damn you, Jake – you will owe me for this." Millicent smiled back. "Okay – load up and start your preflight. I'll wrap up the last of the work. I'll also charge you ten percent on top for this trouble."

"I'll take you to a great hooch-house for an expensive meal next time I'm planet-down. Oh, by the way, you did get the payment that my friend sent you - didn't you?"

"I did, but your hurry-up made the expense a little higher."

The invoice popped up in Jake's ocular-visor, and he approved the cost. His creds plummeted, leaving him 23,000. He grimaced. "That was more than a little. Why not take my balls why you're at it?"

Millicent took out her laser cutter and held it in her hand. "Is that what you want, Jake?"

"How about I just get on board now?" Jake said.

Millicent smiled. "You do that, Jake. Next time you're planet-side, look me up. I'll let you buy me that dinner."

"I'll be sure--"

"And the jar that holds the balls of the dumb-shits that suggest I cut off their balls is all full anyway."

Millicent turned her head so her blond ponytail lashed, laughed a bawdy chuckle, and went back toward Jake's ship.

"Come on, boys – wrap'er up!"

* * *

The fusion powerplant was online and at full capacity. Power to the magnetic compression rings were all green lights… Thrusters, armor, cooling, ammunition, and flightronics all a go. The main engines were online and ready for plasma injection. All readings for the time-space displacement drive were all good.

Jake glanced out the cockpit window. It was Michael hurrying along with a suitcase in his hands.

"Jake, it's Millicent. The last plugs have been removed from the thrusters and engines, and you are a go." Her voice over the comm was damn sexy.

"Permission to come aboard," Michael requested through the comm.

"Permission granted," replied Jake.

Jake heard the external side hatch opening and the lift activating. He fumbled around in a small glass dish. Pulling out a slim device, he poked it into a slot on the cockpit dash.

"Damn Jake, how old is this ship?" Michael asked as he came into the cockpit.

Jake didn't look up from where he was. The redundant systems for the landing gear needed to be vetted. "She's not old – just well-traveled."

"How long is she?"

"Sixty-two meters from nose to glide-fin tips. The cargo hold is eight meters wide. Sleeping compartments are a bit small. This ain't no yacht! It's a workingman's boat."

"All right, skipper – when do we lift the landing gear and cut a hole in the sky? Might I remind you, there is some heat coming?"

"Five more minutes. They're opening the top of the hanger now. We're listed as a test flight, but we're not coming back down. We'll be halfway past the third moon before they figure out we're off this rock."

Jake sat in the pilot's chair. "Michael, you sit there in the copilot's seat." He handed the ship controls over to the ship's autopilot. "All yours, Davy."

"Controls sublet and the ship checks out flight-ready. PTC Valencia, this is the cargo ship H.S. Muncie requesting permission to leave repair hanger 2356 for a test flight to check repairs," Davy said.

"Muncie, you are cleared over-flight and liftoff, PTC," the PTC replied.

"Roger that PTC, Muncie is coming off the deck and have course listing programmed, Muncie," Davy replied.

Outside, Jake saw that all personnel were clear, and the blue warning lights were blinking. The ship shuttered, then came off the ground as the thrusters increased power for the vertical takeoff.

In Jake's ocular-visor, he saw the lane assigned his ship stretching off to the horizon. The actual zero point before his fusion engines could come to bare was out there – in the middle of the mostly-lifeless desert east of the city.

"Davy, copy the plotted course based on PTC sky-path to zero," Jake said.

"Done," Davy replied. "Why?"

"Because."

Jake pushed the thumb trigger on the small electronic device he had on the dash. A flashing light appeared on his quantum comm.

"PTC says we're no longer on their scopes," Davy said. "Did we crash?"

"You'd know if we crashed," Jake said. "We're just running from the law."

"Ah… another narrow escape from local shire reeves," Davy stated.

"Shire reeves?" Michael asked.

"Old – very old-time law men," Jake replied. "We all know you're smart, Davy, don't rub our noses in it." Jake checked his scopes and saw no ships directly approaching, but many in different lanes. "Fly like your ex is looking for you," he added.

"My ex IS looking for me," Davy snapped.

"Muncie 463, are you still in the air? We lost you on our radar. Did you beef? Valencia PTC."

Jake remained cool. He put his feet up and his hands behind his head. "They'll figure out that they don't have any failed instruments in a few minutes, then call the intercept to see if we're a smoking hulk. By then, we'll have nosed-up and kicked our engines into a full burn. They won't know what happened. Just another case of a newly repaired ship having issues with their Q-comm."

They cleared the border walls, and the ship slipped out into the open desert. In the distance were stony hills covered in black, tan, and red striations. Below, a vast plane of tan sand.

"Ready for vertical tilt and engine throttle," Davy said.

"Do so," replied Jake.

The ship tilted nose up, and the whole craft shook as the twin fusion-spike engines put enormous thrust under them. Jake and Michael were pushed back into their seats.

"Don't let yer cock fly up and hit you in the eye," Jake said.

Michael chuckled. "It might fly up and hit YOU in the eye!"

Both men laughed loudly.

There were repeated hails from Valencia PTC as they were climbing higher into the thinning atmosphere. The sky before them grew darker and darker as they got higher up until the planet was vanishing behind them, and the visage of the first of the three moons grew larger.

"Gravity is turned on," Davy said.

Michael got up and walked back toward the cargo bay. "Hey, there's a ship heading this way," he said as he looked out the side window.

Jake came over. "Shit – it's a military ship. My trick doesn't work with them." He ran back to the cockpit. "You'd better take a seat, Michael. Davy, spool up the space-time displacement drive."

"The STDD is up and powered. Also, there is a hostile ship approaching, and their shields are up full front."

Jake jammed in a navkey into the console. "Push us to those coordinates 90 googlewats!"

There was a moment of anxiety and vertigo. All the windows went black, and Jake was sure everything in his mouth tasted like cherry lumpoch.

Michael fell to his knees and gagged a few times, then dry heaved but recovered as he crawled back to his seat. "Yar! Took me around the old Parker Spinner on that one."

"Davy – where did we come out?" Jake asked.

"The three moons and the planet gravity wells lensed us off course by a few AUs. Nothing to get your gumpers in a twist about." The windows cleared. "See – you made it to Callipari 88."

"Okay… let me find the navkey to Paladin," Jake said.

Michael cleared his throat. "Whisky sour if you don't mind, Davy." A small flying drone came from the galley and dropped off the drink in a sippy-glass next to him. He drank some, then looked out on the vast black void and the stark blazes of white fire that dotted the background. "It's been a long time since I sat and looked out on that," he said.

"Found it!" Jake called, just as the whole ship shook, and the sound of compressing metal and tearing erupted.

Chapter 3
Nowhere Like Home

An alarm sounded. Red flashing lights blazed. Jake rushed back to the pilot's chair, jammed the navkey into the slot, and sat down, taking hold of the controls.

"What the tarsus is going on?" Michael shouted.

"Keebler Tinkers—" Jake pushed the thruster controls all forward. "They've got us in an attraction laser, and they're trying to pull us apart!"

"How the hell did they sneak up on us like that?" Michael was on the verge of panic.

"We must have popped out near them. Their ships are covered in meta-materials. Sneaky nogs!"

The ship was growing hot from friction as the stress of the engines fighting against the attraction laser groaned.

"Davy, how far away are they?" Jake called out.

"Fifty-three kilometers, give or take a few klicks... hard to tell really since our scanners only show the equivalent of a tiny cluster of asteroids."

"Then how do you know it's them?" Jake fired back.

"That's where the laser is coming from," Davy said.

"Fire the fusion engines!" Jake yelled.

"Firing all fusion engines," Davy replied.

The ship jerked forward, then the sound of metal tearing and supports giving way was heard. Michael and Jake were pushed back into their seats. Sudden g-forces threw Jake's arms from the controls and into his crotch.

"Son-of-a-bitch that kills!" Jake gritted his teeth. "Davy – it's all up to you – take control."

"One step ahead of you!" Davy stated. "Releasing reflective chaff... Incoming missiles. Deploying holo-decoy with mass generator. Hold on, boys – we're going to make a tight turn..."

Jake felt the blood rushing from his head. His G-protection suit was hard at work, trying to keep him from passing out. "Activate jump to Paladin!"

"Almost ready," Davy said.

The depressurization alarm erupted over the other alarms, and Jake heard the familiar hiss of a pressure breach. The main cabin was venting.

"Coordinates locked and energy is full. Jumping," Davy announced.

Jake was almost unconscious. The windows went black. The hair on his body stood on end, and his ears popped.

"Jake?"

Jake's eyes were coming open. His inner ear hurt, and he felt dehydrated. "What... what happened?"

"You passed out," said Davy.

Jake took stock of himself, then looked over at Michael. A successful jump, he thought.

"We came out one hundred and ten thousand kilometers from the furthest planetary communication buoy."

Struggling to his feet, Jake rubbed his legs to get rid of the pins-and-needle feeling in them. "Michael? You alive or dead?"

"Dead, I think," Michael said as he also got up from his seat. "I'm sure glad those Keebler's didn't get us." He staggered toward the lavatory. "I like the body I have now, certainly wouldn't want it to be parted out for creds. Davy – I need a double whisky after that."

"Coming right up," stated Davy.

"What's the damage?" Jake asked.

"Not good skipper. You know the welds that Millicent's repair team made?"

"Damn it – did they fail?" Jake asked.

"No – those held. The ones around it... not so lucky. The hull-filler gel stopped leaks in the cockpit, but the cargo and living area are now in a vacuum. Can't pump enough air into it to even get a partial pressure," Davy stated.

"Shit!" Jake said. "Okay, based on your best guess, can we make it to an orbiting station and have her repaired?"

"My estimate is that we can actually make it to the planet ship docks, but the evaluation those fix-it-jockeys will tell you might not be good. I think this is going to be really expensive." Davy tried to sound consoling.

"Can the news get any worse?" Jake asked.

"There's a military class frigate hailing us. They picked us up on deep-sweep radar and can see we're damaged. They're asking us if we need assistance," Davy told them.

"Maybe that whisky should be a triple," Michael said as he came out of the head."

Jake took out the ship obfuscator and put it in his pocket. He then put in his own ship's identifier. "Maybe this isn't such a bad thing." He slowed to all-stop and flipped on the comm.

"H.S. Bailiwick, remain stationary at your location. We've detected that your ship has sustained considerable damage. We've deployed a tow-tug to retrieve you. Are you leaking any hazardous byproducts? H.S. Naval Brander Flair over."

"Negative on the hazards, Brander Flair, I think we've only sustained structural damage. We were attacked by Keebler Tinkers on our last hop," Jake replied.

"Prepare for evacuation to our tug, and bring with you all your relevant data stores. Brander Flair out."

* * *

"I'm Captain Lanker, and this is my executive officer Lieutenant Holt, and my Chief, Mister Obart. The Chief has had a look at your ship and has serious doubts that it could survive a planetary entry." Lanker sat back on the couch and took a long drag from his zip-stick. He exhaled a chartreuse-colored mist, then eyed Jake and Michael. "So, Keebler Tinkers tried to snatch you before you jumped here?"

"Yes. We had a failure in the TSD engine, and it

dropped us out in some strange location. When we got it sorted, and our course corrected, the Tinkers were on us. I had to open our fusion drive full to break loose of their attraction laser." Jake took a drink of brandy and put his glass back down on the cocktail table. "We were lucky they were so far away, or that little maneuver I tried would have torn us in half."

"Provide us with the coordinates of your previous location, and we'll send a detachment there to clear out those noggin Keeblers." Lanker sat forward and again took a drag from his zip. "I've contacted the Liebernacht shipyard in orbit around the moon, Tell'in. It's not more than five hundred thousand clicks from here. They're expecting you. If your information on the Keeblers turns out to be accurate, and we make contact – you'll be transferred the bounty for helping the fleet crush another enclave of those damned raiders."

Jake thought for a moment. "Okay, I'm having the location sent to your comm group now."

Lanker was quiet for a moment, then sat back. "We got it. The Host System's Navy thanks you for your assistance in this matter. I'm going to send an escort with you to Liebernacht – to make sure you get there okay."

"We appreciate that," Jake said.

Lanker called over a drone, "Bring us five glasses of Amper Scotch." The small flying drone brought over the drinks, and Lanker raised his glass.

"Here's to calm seas and a safe voyage."

* * *

The engineer in charge of repairs at the Liebernacht shipyard came over to Jake and Michael, all the while shaking his head. "I can't believe that held together while being towed here. Plus, that hulk is a hundred years old – I can't believe you fly around in it."

"One man's junk is another's treasure," Jake replied.

"You're one brave soul – or insane," the engineer

stated.

"Just let me know what it'll cost to fix it," Jake said.

"You'd be better off selling her for scrap. Wait a second, my head fusion manager is sending me a note." The engineer was quiet for a minute. "Ah – your power supply is in good shape. That's a plus. Oh -and most of your flight gear is still in decent shape. But, your structural rating is shot to shit. The landing gear, gone. Heat shielding is discontinuous now, and your compression integrity is nonexistent in all but the cockpit."

Jake fostered a weak smile. "Not entirely terrible."

The engineer chuckled. "I admire your notion of terrible. You must be an optimist. I'll have a full damage report for you in a couple of days."

"A couple of days?"

"I have a ton of work on my plate, and a small ship like yours is not high on the priority list – but we'll get to her. I can assure you if it can be repaired, we'll get 'er done. If she can't, we'll pay you the best price to part her out and scrap her."

Jake felt uneasy at the prospect of losing his ship. "Here's my Q-comm public code. Send all messages here. We'll be on Paladin. How often do shuttles leave for planet-side?"

"Every two hours. There's also jammers who can take you, but it isn't free," the engineer said.

"We'll wait," Michael said.

"Head to the waiting-concourse and have some refreshments. You can also take a quick course on Paladin customs and laws – just so you don't end up in trouble," the engineer stated.

"Much appreciated," Jake replied, then headed toward the door and into the public areas of the shipyard."

Jake and Michael waited around for the shuttle. Once it arrived, they had to wait for the passengers to disembark. Once onboard, the seats were comfortable, and there were drinks and a meal offered on the flight down to the Delany Space Port.

It was many years since Jake had his feet on the surface of Paladin. There was a flood of emotions running through his mind and heart as the craft descended into the atmosphere.

The shuttle quaked as the craft smashed into the upper mesosphere. Fire was all around them. This lasted only a minute, then they were slowing and cooling. Soon, Jake would be standing on the surface – and he'd have to at last deal with his own feelings of his youth.

A steward-bot came by offering drinks. Jake took a large glass of ambrosia-fisk – a local Paladin liquid drug that makes the user lose all sense of anxiety and feel hyper-conscious.

"Passengers – this is your pilot speaking. We're sixty-two miles above Delany Space Port. The time of arrival is twenty minutes. Please have your visa chips set to on, and let the steward-bot know if you need anything special before landing."

Advertisements began to play over the common communication channel, and Jake switched his off. He looked over at Michael sitting next to him and noted the expression of pure unabashed delight flush over his face.

"You should switch that shit off," Jake said.

"No! Not until I learn what I can do with a pango-frog…" Michael stated.

"You'd better leave that shit alone – you'll get warts," Jake replied.

Michael chuckled. "Probably not the worst thing to catch on this planet."

The shuttle made landfall, and the ramps were connected to the exit doors. Three dozen people wandered into the holding area. A que formed as passengers briefly halted at customs to allow their visa chip to execute its complex quantum-based program.

Once in the duty-free commercial zone, Jake hurried

toward the exit and the flycars. All around were shops selling drugs, entertainment, exotic food, and sex of all sorts. His eye caught the neon glow of the Haymaker Torture Palace. Jake knew what went on in such places, for in his youth, one of his friends was consigned to it for the pleasures of incoming tourists. He never saw him again. The thought made his stomach churn.

Most of those he knew when a youth had died many Paladin years ago, their lives ripped to pieces by a form of slavery too terrible to think about. Jack was lucky, he'd found a source of ForeTran660. That drug provided a hoard of nanobots into the user to repair and roll back the human aging process. He never regretted stealing a hypo of it and injecting himself.

"Hey – let's stop in here," Michael said.

"Later. First a temp-flat, then you can sate your base desires," Jake stated as they found the numo-tube and went down to the flycar pick-up zone. "Where we heading?"

Michael chuckled. "Not sure. Last known location for Peter Long -."

Jake laughed. "What – really? That's the guy's name?"

"Can I finish?" Michael asked. "Peter Long was last identified at 26897 Ridgefield Rout, Clover Dale Glen, in the Hamptonshire Zone."

"Then, we'll have to book a country inn. That location is quite rural," Jake said.

"Rural? Have you been here before?" Michael asked.

Jake grunted. "I've been lots of places."

"Jake, ol' friend – you surprise me every time we speak," Michael stated, then gave a hearty laugh while slapping him on the back.

Once outside in the open air, Jake found a skycar for rent, and he and Michael climbed in. Michael said where they wanted to go, and Jake added they needed to find an inn. The car accelerated into the sky, then headed south.

The ride was subsonic, making it to Clover Dale in a

little over three hours. The car descended and gingerly placed Jake and Michael at the front parking lot of the Labor's Lost Inn. But, to call it a quaint county inn would be a misrepresentation – for it was once a lordly manor house, now turned into a vast six hundred room hotel.

Jake booked the rooms on his way in and made sure they got one at ground level. The cost was not significant – since the hotel made most of its money from activities that did not include sleeping.

Approaching the counter, Jake asked, "Do you happen to know how we can get out to 26897 Ridgefield Rout?"

The young lady behind the counter nodded. "It's a slim-joint down off Highway 35, just ask a groundpounder to take you there."

Groundpounder – Jake knew the term well, and the word slim-joint. Anxiety was creeping in on him. He was more than uncomfortable. "We'll do that. Thanks," he muttered.

The girl looked at Jake and Michael – there was an almost unabashed look in her eye. "Enjoy your stay," she said and sent the key code to their personal inboxes.

Chapter 4
Best Laid Plans of Aliens and Men

Drawn by horses, the ornate country coaches still plied the dirt and gravel roads of Clover Dale. But, not far from them, a modern two-lane highway allowed groundpouders, six-wheeled high-speed conveyances, to get from one place to another with far more efficiency.

The groundpounder trundled along at a fair pace, the large thousand-acre farms speeding by. Jake stared out – his mind lost in a world three hundred years past.

"We should take one of those carriages for a ride," Michael said.

Jake glanced over. He did not want to interact with this culture or society any more than he had to. "Let's keep things as brief as possible here."

"Okay." Michael reached for the food dispenser and got out a sandwich. "You should eat something – might make you less of a cranky asshole."

Jake chuckled. "You may be right." He pressed a few buttons, then acknowledged the price in his ocular-visor. A hot pastry popped out of the dispenser.

The groundpounder took a side road, and the craft began to slow. In the distance, there was a set of warehouses – large and looming over the landscape like so many travel trunks strewn about a space port entry dock.

The road bifurcated, and the groundpounder took a leisurely left toward one building. Autonomous transports and tool-bots were all about. Jake and Michael rolled onto a wide area laid flat and covered in asphalt.

"Your destination has been reached. Please watch your head as you exit the vehicle," said the groundpounder. "If you wish me to stay while you do your task, I am quite willing to hold and charge you."

Jake got out. "Yes, stay here. We shouldn't be long."

Michael led the way into the two-story office building.

A prominent sign read, Gunderson and Son's C-Meat, Inc.

A tall man with long blond hair greeted them at the door. "Michael!" he said, "I'm Donald Newt. I'm here to take you to Mister Long." He turned and walked through the automatic doors.

Michael and Jake followed. The open reception was brightly lit, with a sizeable half-arc information counter manned by two amazingly beautiful women and two unnaturally handsome men.

"What is it you make here?" Michael asked.

Jake came up alongside and said just above a whisper, "They produce cultured-meats."

Donald glanced over his shoulder. "We produce some of the finest foods creds can purchase. We supply any form of meat you care to think of to all the best establishments here on Paladin and afar."

They came to a numo-tube and went up to the second floor. The carpeting in the hall was showing a top-down view from some sky-high perspective. As they walked, underfoot, puffy clouds appeared and then floated away with each fleeting step.

Donald stopped and motioned for them to enter an office. The doors parted, and both Michael and Jake went in. The door closed, and they were standing in front of an old-style polished wood desk with two hover-lamps on the front corners. On the desk, in the middle, was a vase with a lid. But, there was no one else in the room.

"Where's Peter?" Michael asked.

"He's there at his desk," replied Donald.

A queasy feeling came over Jake. "In the urn?"

"Precisely," said Donald.

Jake turned and was immediately impressed with the type of firearm he saw. "A Grover Klink 17," Jake said.

"You have a good eye for weapons," Donald stated.

Michael did not turn but walked over to the desk and looked down on the urn. "Peter, you stroid-joker son-of-a-bitch," he said. He turned and looked at Donald. "So, why the hook-pipe?"

Donald looked down at the gun. "I need to know that we're all friends before I put this away. Before Long died, he asked me to help one of his pals. He asked me to give you this." Donald tossed a plastic pouch to Jake.

Jake tossed the pouch to Michael. "He was your friend," he added.

Michael opened the envelope and took out three sugar-cube size crystals.

Donald cleared his throat. "He also told me what they're for. I know you're going after the Solomon Lake Treasure. And, now, you have a partner."

"Okay – there's enough for the three of us," Michael said. "You don't have to throw the ball-rocker on us."

"What say you?" Donald asked Jake.

Jake gave a sigh. "Well, threes company, and four's an orgy. Welcome aboard – partner."

Donald tucked the pistol into his belt. "You two have been standing here, slack-jawed for almost two minutes, and neither of you has asked what happened to Mister Long."

"We had other concerns," Jake stated. "How'd he die?"

"Killed a few days ago in his home. The place was turned upside down. Whoever it was, might have been looking for those crystals."

"How do you fit into this again?" Michael asked.

"Five weeks ago, Mister Long came to me, worried. He asked me to keep something for him."

"The crystals," Jake said.

Donald nodded. "Exactly. On the day that he was being murdered, he sent me a note telling me to keep an eye out for your arrival and why." Donald let out a slight chuckle. "Whatever killed him took his head. There were no other transmissions from him other than the one to me. Local authorities are still looking for his head to get the last data from his cortex-implants."

"You cremated the rest?" Michael asked.

"Indeed so, per his request," replied Donald. "Now, what's our next step?"

"Since we have the where and the how, we might as well get back to our ship and wait for the repairs to be completed," Jake said.

"Good. I'll take a leave of absence from here and ride with you two." He walked over and took the three cubs from Michael. "Until we get there – I'll hold on to these."

"Come on, fellas – what's the hurry?" Michael asked. "Let's live a bit. There's lots of sights and things to do here… drugs, booze, sexual things only I can dream of."

Donald scrutinized Jake and Michael.

"Look, Michael, this isn't the time to trip down the wanky-lanky," Jake said. "When you've got the slather in your paw, and your cred limit is blue, and all the javy-naves are coming to you for some cutter, you can come back here to debase yourself. For now, let's get somewhere a crazed head-lopping maniac can't easily get us."

Michael seemed to come to his senses. "Ah… the head-lopper. Good thinking, Jake ol' boy. Definitely don't want my head tossed in a bin. Let's get the nog out of here – and spare no expense!"

Jake nodded. He'd kept Donald in his peripheral vision and noted the man nod slightly in agreement. "We have a groudpounder waiting outside," Jake said.

Donald chuckled. "Why roll along the ground when we can just take the corporate ship to wherever your craft is at?"

Jake paid for the groundpounder's time and closed his connection to it. He indicated with his hand for them to head out. "Lead on, Donald me lad."

They took a numo-tube to an executive suite on the roof. There was an exceptionally expensive spacecraft on the roof-pad.

"I've never been checked out on one of these," Jake said, surprised at the beauty and elegance of the ship. "Do we need a pilot?"

"The AI is fully checked out. Quadruple redundancy on all systems. And, if we had to go to manual, I'm licensed to fly it," Donald said.

"What is it you do here?" Jake asked.

"Security Operation Executive for all Gunderson and Son's C-Meat, Inc. facilities on Paladin," Donald replied as they approached the boarding hatch and climbed in.

The seats were covered in dark red felt, and the walls were currently showing the external view. It appeared that they were floating just above the landing pad.

Donald sat down. "Take a seat, fellas. Pilot, take us to…" He smiled and gestured to Jake to continue.

"Liebernacht Shipyard," Jake proclaimed.

Over the innercom, a voice spoke. "Mister Newt, you have the authority to direct this ship wherever you wish. Setting course and flight plan to Liebernacht Shipyard. In the meantime, the servicebots will be by to provide anything you may wish, including sexual services. Settle in and enjoy your flight."

The ship floated above the pad, then nosed up and accelerated at tremendous speed. In short order, the planet grew smaller at the aft, and the first moon was passed on the port side as they sped toward Liebernacht.

They were twenty kilometers from Liebernacht when the AI began the deceleration. The Space Traffic Control (STC) from Liebernacht called, and the AI handled all the docking procedures. The hanger doors closed, and all three men were walking toward a numo-tube as they headed to the lobby.

"I'll get us some rooms," Jake said, then connected his comm system to the shipyard client-hosting facilities. Three rooms were easy to secure, and he paid in advance. He also checked on the repairs and then headed to the bar.

Michael waved him over to a set of seats against a thick alumina-glass window. The view of the stars and semi-empty space was spectacular. "I ordered us some push-pulls, and some steaks with pluteus mushroom gravy," he said.

"Those mushrooms can mess a man's mind up, but that gravy is to die for." Jake's mouth began to salivate at the thought.

Donald just sat there, quiet, observing the near-empty bar. "How long before your ship is good to go?"

Jake sat back and put his free arm up on the back of the chair next to him. "Seventy-two hours. They had to print some components that were torn beyond welding. Anyway, not too long."

Donald nodded. Michael looked out the window as an autobot came with the drinks and food.

Jake took the napkin and gingerly dabbed the corners of his mouth. "Damn fine meal. A good choice, Michael," he said.

Michael nodded. "We'd better retreat back to our rooms before the gravy kicks in. This should help us pass the next couple of days."

Donald chuckled. "I could use the diversion." He stood up and brushed off the front of his pants. "See you boys when the gravy wears off." Turning, he left the bar and was gone.

Jake watched him leave, then he turned back. "So, what do you think?"

Michael seemed lost in thought. "There's something not right with that guy," he mumbled.

"I agree. Don't trust him too much," Jake told Michael. "When we get to the treasure, we'll need to be doubly on our guard."

Jake secured the door to his room, then laid down on the bed. The gravy hit him with a strong wave of heat over his entire body. Wave after wave washed over him as if he was roasting in one of the pits of Trudo, the volcanic moon circling Paladin.

After a few minutes, he heard voices singing in perfect

harmony, followed by the shadows of the room becoming quivering beasts. Colors became a statement of his emotional mindset. Lust and rage came upon him slowly, as he considered ordering a lover for his sleep-period. Then, it changed.

Jake wept bitter tears as he struggled with the reality of his own past. "Why did you leave me there!" he shouted – and felt better for it.

His mind wandered, and in the darkness of his despair, a white light appeared. He was floating. All his anxieties and sadness fell away.

Am I dead?

He was high above a desert landscape, the sky, an azure vision.

His nudity did not seem odd, and he became aware that he was slowly descending. Below was a strange sight. Tan rocky outcroppings made up of colorful striations like a layer cake.

All around, covering the ground was white sand, as if an armada of ships carrying refined sugar broke apart and spread their contents over the surface. There was a voice, and it was getting closer.

"Into the realm. Live, love, and be one with me," the voice said.

Jake was straining to hear. Was it a woman, a man… an alien? He could not tell yet, but the words were distinct.

Below him, the sound of rushing water was growing louder. Now he was no more than five or six hundred feet above the ground. There were unnatural depressions in the rocks. Where the tan stone came to the surface of the sugar-white, there was a rectangular opening. He saw water flowing in channels along walls that were holding back the sugar.

"Who are you?" shouted Jake. "What am I doing here?"

"Live, love, and be one with me," repeated the voice.

He was now a hundred feet off the deck and

anticipating that his bare feet would touchdown on the top of one of the walls that enclosed a courtyard and a bright grassy space.

There was a sense of unmeasured anticipation. Absent was all anxiety and fear. Inside the courtyard at one end were columns holding up a portico leading into darkness and the ground. All along the top of the wall was a channel that carried crystal-clear water rapidly tumbling and churning.

He wanted to search this place – his heart was telling him he was home… this was his home. Almost down - his toes about to touch the top of the smooth stone wall. His desire to get into the courtyard – feel the grass below his feet – to explore the inside of this spectacular place was overwhelming.

Then, he began to rise.

"No, not now! Down – not up!" Jake called out. "No, no, no!" He rose so fast into the white light that it forced his eyes open.

Jake woke. He was naked lying on the floor. His mouth was dry, and he struggled to get to his feet. He stumbled to the food dispenser and asked for water and a wake-patch. He drank down the liquid and slapped the patch on his upper arm. His heart raced, and the jolt to full awareness was both startling and irreversible.

Jake went back to his bed, sat down, and accessed his ocular-visor. Two messages from the repair engineer. One was asking permission to update the AI pilot. The second was thanking for permission to update the AI pilot software and telling him that the work was done.

He sent a message to Michael. "Michael, I don't know how long I was out, but now I'm awake, and the repairs are done. Did you give permission to update the AI? Anyway, let's get the nog out of here!"

Michael replied. "I'm ready to float in the ink. And, what's this about the AI? I'll meet you in the lobby."

Chapter 5
No Other

The ship lurched out beyond the gravity wells of the solar system. Jake, Michael, and Donald were sitting around the small utility table. The new AI copilot was keeping them posted on their preparations to jump to the navkey coordinates.

"We are cleared to make the jump. The coordinates are processed, and the six-way movement is plotted. You may want to hold on to your butts since this will be an uncharted location," Davy stated.

There was a whining sound as the STD drive ramped up. The windows went black, and they waited.

After twenty minutes, Donald got up and went to the head. Michael retrieved a couple of zip-sticks and handed one to Jake.

"I know that everything passes through time as one of the angles of travel, but this is a ridiculous amount of time we're... traveling," Michael said as he drew in the sweet vapor. "Damn, that really opens up the lungs."

Jake spoke calmly. "When I was in the navy, some of our jumps took a few hours."

"Well, I don't like it," Michael said. "And, I never knew you were in the navy."

"Davy, how long did you estimate this passage to take?" Jake asked.

"Fifty-five minutes. On the galactic map, the destination is at the very edge of one of the spiral arms. There is no record of the endpoint being charted by private, governmental, or military sources," Davy told them.

Donald stepped back into the connecting hall just in front of the airlock that led to the docking chamber. He went to the food dispenser and ordered a coffee and a donut. Sitting on the edge of one of the bottom bunks, he watched both Jake and Michael. "So, we're still in travel mode?"

"Still," Jake told him.

"Quite the dark-wave, if you ask me," Michael said.

Donald stood up and sat in an auxiliary seat behind the pilot's chair. "What are you going to do with your share – when you monetarize it?"

Michael thought for a moment. "Buy my own planet. Probably a one-G somewhere and throw global parties until they can't replace any of my organs anymore."

"You, Jake?" Donald asked.

"Build a ship and Captain Nemo around the galaxy. Might even travel to the next galaxy over and see what's there," Jake replied.

Donald drank down his coffee and finished his donut. "When you say, 'Captain Nemo', do you mean you'll sink war ships as you float about?"

Jake chuckled. "Ah – I'd forgotten about that part of the story. You know what I mean – just be free and do my own thing. Don't get hassled by any badge-baggers or bummers."

"How's that different than now?" Donald asked.

"I'd be less likely to starve when in port, and when I feel the need for some touch, I won't get the ruffy-rags, but the finest shimmer-shown only," Jake said.

"How about you?" Michael asked.

"I'm not counting my turtles before they're hatched," Donald stated. "We don't know that the items are there, or if they're accessible, or even real. I'll reserve my fantasy for after we load up."

Davy came over the ship's intercom. "I'm preparing deep scans for when we arrive. Seven minutes until we pop out.

Jake got up and retrieved a suka – a refreshing drink made from ragea berries and carbonated water. He sat back down in the pilot's seat and sipped his beverage.

The ship shook, and the widows became translucent again.

"Scan sent," Davy announced. "Contact – multiple unidentified ships."

Jake choked on his suka. "What… ships?"

"Also, asteroids - the smallest of which is ten kilometers wide and a kilometer deep. Thickness varies from a few kilometers to a hundred kilometers," Davy called out.

"Put us in the shadow of one of those chunks of rock!" Jake shouted.

"Already in process," Davy said. "I'm using attitude thrusters to keep our signature low."

"They'll know we hit them with a hard scan," Donald said.

"As long as they don't give us a hard scan back," Michael quipped.

"Any activity?" Jake asked.

"None yet. I think all the debris around us masked our deep scan. Hopefully, they think it was an anomaly… depending on what they are," Davy stated.

The ship ducked into the gravitational well of a large asteroid. "I'm going to land on it," Davy said.

The AI copilot brought them in and set them down on the rocky surface of the behemoth mass of floating rock. Davy tucked them behind a projection and just within a depression on the surface.

"I've sent out a drone to peek over the lip of this hill and watch for any activity," Davy said.

"What were the ranges on the various contacts?" Jake asked.

"Fifty thousand klicks for five of the big ships. Thirty thousand klicks for three of the smaller ships. Twenty thousand klicks for the medium-size ships," Davy said. I have images too."

Over the small holo-table appeared the ships. The largest class of craft was fifteen kilometers long and shaped like a tapered hollow tube. Next was composed of multiple orbs tied together, this was the medium class, and it was four kilometers in circumference. The smallest class measured just under a kilometer in length and half that in width. From the smallest ship emerged even smaller craft that swarmed about.

"Colonial ships?" Donald hypothesized.

"Whoever they are, they're standing directly in the way of our booty," Michael said.

"Perhaps they'll move on soon?" Jake mused.

"Probably not very soon," Davy said. "They seem to be chopping up asteroids and processing them in one of the large ships. Definitely, some type of colonial fleet. Wait… we're being hit with a high-powered scan array."

The ship was vibrating. Debris was floating up from where the Bailiwick was sitting.

"Wow – that electromagnetic wave had the force of a few giganewtons…nice," Davy announced. "Ah – now some of the smaller ships are coming this way."

"Davy – cut all power, excluding life-necessary systems," Jake said.

"Aye-aye skipper," Davy replied. "They're using radio frequency communication for local comms."

"Put it in our ears," Jake commanded.

Across each man's comm, there was a series of rapid clicks and hisses. In some cases, there was an odd lip-smacking sound.

"Pipe it into the translator system," Jake commanded.

"Will do," replied Davy.

"Do you think it's coded?" Michael asked.

"We'll know in short order," Donald added.

They sat around waiting. Jake got some food and drink from the dispensary, then sat on one of the bunks. Michael flipped on his galactic-media implant and began watching a show on Solomon Lake. Donald quietly waited.

An hour passed. Jake watched the scanner data

closely. The strange alien ships came close – within fifty kilometers of their position. Around the Bailiwick, the odd scanning wave churned up dust and debris. Finally, the drone recorded the ships pulling away.

Further and further, the aliens fell away. The active scanning of their position stopped, and the passive scanner showed the crafts were growing more distant.

"I have a partial translation from the alien chatter," Davy said.

"Give it to me," Jake told the AI.

"Now – you understand that the amount of translation and the complexity of the linguistic sentence construction will make this a best guess as to meaning – right?" Davy stated.

"Stop stalling and give it to us!" Jake demanded.

"Okay – here it is. Translation part one – ten minutes and seven seconds into monitoring: 'Far way, send search next violet'. Second translation twenty-two minutes and forty seconds: 'Anomaly repeated not. Heat two orange slither'. Third translation at sixty-one minutes and nineteen seconds: 'Anomaly not repeated. Return to primary mission'," Davy said. "I'll continue to analyze as we continue on."

"Okay, keep me posted on your analysis," Jake ordered. "I think we can move slowly and use minimal thrusters now—no active scanning. We'll just listen for the aliens to ping us. Recall the drone. Davy, take us out and head toward the treasure location."

Jake took his seat at the pilot controls, Michael sat in the co-pilot seat, and Donald sat at the navigation station. The ship slowly rose from the asteroid surface, and ever-so-slowly headed toward where the aliens had been.

"I see minor distortions of light against the star. Appears to be small debris like objects where the alien fleet was," Davy announced.

"Do a soft scan, just enough energy to give us a picture," Jake ordered.

A moment passed, then Davy came back on over the comm. "Definitely debris, with some organics mixed in. I'm reading polymer strands encasing bio-material, and some organic masses exposed to vacuum."

"Stay our course," Jake said.

"Alien material and objects of unknown origin could be quite profitable for this crew if we were to gather it and report it when returning to human-occupied space," Davy stated.

"Noted," Jake replied. "Now, take us to that treasure."

Davy flew the ship along a varied course, staying in the scan-shadow of large asteroids and among the magnetic field of reacting solar wind regions.

It took a few hours of maneuvering to reach the near planetoid object that created most of the gravity well of the region. On the surface, at a set of precise coordinates, was the treasure of Solomon Lake.

They slowly descended. There was such little atmosphere on the planetoid there was no burn from resistance upon entry.

"There are signs of other landings here. Some radiation imprints too. Might be uranium below the surface..." Davy said. The ship landed softly. "Gravity is 1.53 percent of standard."

"There –" Jake pointed at the scanner data and chuckled. "That cavern is not natural. He was an old pirate, alright."

"What do you mean?" Michael asked.

"It's an old pirate trick – and miners used it too in the old days. Make yourself a nuke of about one megaton yield. Bury it at the correct distance from the surface of a solid material object and detonate it. The resulting bubble of molten material will create a dome cavern. Where the bubble burst through the surface, typically leaves an access way," Jake explained.

"What about the radiation. A fission explosion

leaves plenty of residue behind," Michael added.

"Remember that Solomon had mining and construction bots with him. He could have found a source of boron and made some boron carbide to coat the inside walls. By now, the half-life should have rendered the radiation negligible anyway."

"Good," Michael said with a smile. "So, what? Drones leading the way as we enter?"

"Sounds like a reasonable approach," Donald said.

"Davy, we're going out. Mind the store and release a drone to map the passage ahead of us," Jake commanded.

"Aye-aye," Davy said. "I'll monitor your progress and be prepared to get out of here at a moment's notice."

"Can't ask for much else," Jake replied.

Chapter 6
Where Fools Dare

The Drone was slowly moving and scanning the passageway a few hundred meters ahead of them. The entrance was jagged, like a gaping maw of some horrific monster. There were places where the liquid rock had bubbled and burst, leaving black, half-egg shapes, cracked, and broken on the ends.

It was clear from the images that there was a paved path that started a hundred meters in. From there, a structure was built big – tall and wide corridors with no apparent airlocks or doors.

On their ocular-visors, they watched the drone make its way to a set of stairs and descended for some time. Walls were smooth, like polished iron, and the stairs appeared to be made of white marble.

The drone scanned with x-rays and laser scanners – no traps appeared, and no personal spaces were found. Radiation was low, almost normal for full exposure in a vacuum.

After some time, the drone came to a level corridor. At the end, a door bared the craft's path. Attempted x-ray scanning provided no information – as the door seemed to be immune to the drone's efforts.

"Alright, lets head in," Jake said.

They filed out of the airlock – three Tandyman vac suits brightly colored against the backdrop of gray and black stone. Each man picked his way around the broken lava bubbles and jagged rocks left over from the nuke's star-furnace heat. Into the cavernous opening, they each went.

It took a half-hour to reach the still hovering drone. The door was large – ten meters wide and twenty tall. The thickness was unknown.

"Okay – now what?" Michael asked.

"Donald – this is your bit," Jake said.

Unzipping his pocket, Donald brought forth the three cubes. "Now, we just need to know where to jam them, then we're golden."

"Come on – search the surface of the door. Most likely, there's a hatch that has controls for these memory cubes," said Jake.

From top to bottom, they searched. There were no seams – only a polished flat surface.

"Alright, take one of the crystals and move it over the surface. Maybe there's a hidden scanner or something that will unlock the door," Jake said.

Donald took the crystals and slid the cubes over the surface of the door. Still – nothing happened.

"What about this?" Michael said from behind them. He'd found a small metal plate nearly invisible along the corridor. He pushed it inward, and the small hatch slid down, exposing three cube-shaped spaces.

"Michael – you lively donker!" Jake said. "Donald – plug your cubes in there, and let's see what happens."

Donald walked over. He slipped in one, another, then the last. Nothing happened.

"Is there a button or some controls we need to push?" Michael asked.

Taking the cubes out, Donald switched their position. The door pushed out, then rotated 90 degrees, then slid back into the darkness and vanished.

Beyond the doorframe, lights lining the walls came on, illuminating a long corridor much like the one behind them.

"Davy, send the drone beyond the doorway," Jake commanded.

The drone sped off into the unknown, all the while relaying images from its scanners. Hallway, lights, stairs, more hallway – the images abruptly stopped.

"Davy, what happened?" Jake asked.

"Not sure. Analyzing the telemetry information

and last comm transaction now. Ah – a powerful laser hit the drone. It was most likely valorized," Davy said.

"Send down another drone," Jake ordered.

"On its way. Note – we only have three left," Davy stated.

"Set it for combat intelligence behavior," Jake said.

"Already done," Davy answered.

The craft came and hovered next to Jake, then moved off down the hallway.

"The drone has deployed ground-rollers. I'm gathering the data now. Trigger points for the defense system are identified. Wow – look at those tools -," Davy told them.

In Jake's ocular-visor, he saw three mining lasers in a large warehouse. All three devices were pointed at the entrance. The ground-rollers scurried about watching, recording, and watching the industrial devices as they scanned the area searching for threats.

"That Solomon Lake was a clever son-of-a-bitch," Donald said.

"Davy, send in a ground-roller to disable the three lasers. Send the others to recon the warehouse," Jake commanded.

"We're taking account now," Davy replied. "Mining and construction equipment. Crates and containers – all sealed and locked. Scanners and viewers. Hey, look at this!"

Jake saw a spacecraft sitting in the middle, surrounded by cargo containers and crates. It was twice as big as Jake's ship, with modular attachment ports for connecting extra carrying containers to its hull.

"Must be one of Solomon's ships…" Jake mused.

"Lasers are disabled. You are cleared to enter," Davy announced.

"Rollers report that the warehouse is sixty-five thousand square feet of storage space. Most of it is empty.

There are life support systems and convenience-kiosks of the old style in the back. Plenty of food and potable water is also on site. The roof is a bit odd. I'll send the drone to look," Davy said.

Jake, Michael, and Donald made their way down the hall. At the entrance to the warehouse, they found a dark mark on the wall and ceiling – the remains of the previous drone.

They stepped into the warehouse – massive steel supports held up a complex of cross beams and roof supports. Looked as though sheets of steel made up the covering at the very top. Hanging down were powerful fixtures that illuminated the entire space in bright white light.

The floor appeared to be some sort of cement, poured in large sections, and polished to a lustrous shine.

"The ground-rollers have connected me to all known control systems in this place," Davy said. "Some encryption models are being used here – but they're pretty old. I've already ciphered them. Can you believe it?"

"Excellent! Gather all the date and manifests and let me know what we're dealing with here," Jake said.

"It's a hodge-podge of information. Ah – here's what you're looking for. Alien artifacts in order of size," Davy said. "He's kindly cataloged the items, and they are all in three containers. Clearly, Solomon did not know what they do or why they could be important. He states in one place, 'it could be a garbage compactor for all I know'." Not very helpful, I'm afraid."

"Davy, direct us to the three containers that have the alien tech," Jake requested.

A translucent orange line appeared superimposed over the floor, leading them to their target.

"I'm uploading Solomon's navigation data. There are some interesting details therein," Davy said.

It took a few minutes, but they finally arrived at three large containers sitting side by side.

"Open the containers," Jake commanded.

The three containers popped their seals at the same time. Swinging open, the lights came on inside. Smaller boxes were within.

Jake took one and set it on the cement floor. There was a crypto-lock. "Davy, can you open this for us?"

"Sure – just read me the small set of letters and numbers on the box," Davy replied.

Jake did, and the smaller box popped its lid. He pulled out the items one by one and laid them on the floor.

A golden disk, a cylinder with tendrils, two orbs linked by some force, and a small silver cube made up the items.

"Looks like crap," Michael said. "Let's pull out something else."

Donald went in and brought out a slightly larger box. Jake read off the lock number, and Davy opened it.

Taking out a crystal-clear container of black goo, Donald looked at Jake and Michael and shrugged his shoulders. "Hell if I know," he said. He set it on the floor, then dipped his hands back into the box.

Out came three fist-sized mushroom-shaped objects. Donald reached in again and pulled forth some textiles and then an oblong-shaped bronze-colored ring.

"Great – we've become the proud owners of a crap-heap," Michael added. "We'd be better off collecting that floating garbage those aliens dumped."

"Patience, lad," Jake said. "We're digging now…who knows what we'll find in there?"

"I suggest we load it all up in the ship and sort it out at a secure hanger someplace," Donald replied.

Jake nodded. "Good idea. Davy, we're going to bring out some shipping containers. Open the rear hatch when we emerge."

"Will do, Jake," Davy said.

Jake suddenly had a strange feeling deep down in

his gut. *Davy never calls me by my first name... he thought. What's he up to?*

Slowly, they moved the containers along the corridors, up the stairs, and to the mouth of the cavern. One by one, they put the mighty boxes in and secured them. Once they were all inside, they went back in to investigate the rest of the warehouse.

In the far back, there was a mezzanine with a set of rooms, one stacked atop the other. Jake went up and found a control room.

"Davy, can you connect to this control room?" Jake asked.

"I'm connected. What do you want to know – Jake?"

"Davy – 1087," Jake said.

"Hello, skipper – you've activated personality two of the AI module. You must be in deep shit. I'm now on a secure connection," Davy said. "From what personality one has detailed, you're in deep trouble."

"What the nog do you mean?" Jake asked.

"Where's Donald? Do you see him anywhere?" Davy asked.

Jake looked around. "No – what's this about?"

"Here's his location," Davy said and put a three-dimensional map on his ocular-visor. The holographic avatar of Donald was nearly to the exit of the cavern. "He's nogged us..." Jake said. "Connect me to Michael, encrypted."

"What's the haps?" Michael asked.

"Donald is nearly to the ship," Jake said.

"Son-of-a-bitch!" Michael swore. "Tell Davy to not take off and lock the ship."

"Davy, can you – " Jake got out.

"Sorry, skipper – but that upgrade they did over-wrote my admin controls. Donald has all the authority."

"Except module sixteen that Millicent added to your code," Jake interjected.

"What's module sixteen?" Michael asked.

Jake rushed toward the exit. "In case of a legit authority attempting to lock out the ship's AI. There is one aspect of Davy that they wouldn't know about, and it would remain hidden from the whole personality when they re-launched the system."

"I wouldn't try to leave, Jake," Davy said. "He's re-enabled the mining lasers. They're looking for movement at the portal."

"Can you shut them down?" Jake asked.

"Sorry, all I can do regarding this ship is to keep you apprised of Donald's actions and our movements. I'm just advising at this stage," Davy replied.

"So, how the fuck do we get out of here?" Jake asked.

"Funny story," Davy began, "that room with all the controls actually opens the hanger bay doors. That old ship of Solomon's probably still works."

"Fly that thing?" Jake's voice was filled with doubt.

"Either that or wait for rescue. Could be weeks or even years, depending on if they destroy me once we're back in human space," Davy said.

"You can't be considering that as an option," Michael told Jake.

"What choice do we have? Okay, Davy, we're going to take her up. Can you download to me the flight manual and engineering information?" Jake asked.

"Already done, Jake," Davy replied.

"Hey – did you say that a legit authority tampered with your ship?" Michael asked.

"Donald must be working for the Host Systems," Jake said. "Only they'd have the ability to knock out my administrative access."

Michael came up to Jake and grabbed him by the arms. "We're humped, lad!"

Jake brushed off Michael's hands. "Keep your

continence! That bastard may have my ship and our loot, but he made a serious mistake."

"What? He didn't nuke us in here?" Michael asked, sarcasm heavy in his voice.

"In a way. He fucked up by not killing us," Jake said. "That leaves us a slim chance of getting our alien tech back."

Jake headed toward the centuries-old space craft. He looked up into the superstructure of the ceiling. "I hope that roof opens," he said. "Davy, open the rear hatch of this thing and start helping me do the preflight. I see it has a Mark III fusion powerplant. I hope it will still work."

Chapter 7
Flight of the Silver Horn

Jake climbed into Solomon's ship. The first thing he saw was something that did not belong on a human spaceship.

"What in the hell is that thing?" Michael asked.

"Nogged if I know," Jake said. "But it's tied into this solid-state computer."

"An SSC? How old is this crap-nugget?" Michael shook his head. "Those damn things went out with murdering animals for food."

"Davy, what are these extra things attached to the ship?" Jake asked.

"Can't tell you," Davy replied. "Appears that Solomon Lake was attaching some of the alien tech to his own ship."

"Alien tech... Of course it would be attached to the only escape ship we have," Jake grumbled.

"You're going to need to fire up the reactor. Once it's producing, we can determine what the other systems need – and do," Davy stated.

Jake found the fusion engine. Following the engineering instructions, he got all green lights on the control console. "It's up and running."

"Good! Now head to the midsection and open panels L through P. There will be a fiber interface where you can connect your ocular-visor into. I'll try and help mediate the communication between this bucket of bolts and your implants," Davy said.

"Good enough. All I ask is that I get a shot at that bastard before he links up with the Host System Guarda," Jake said.

"Ah – he's not doing that. He's asked personality one to take him to Philbeen 9. I think he's double-crossing the Host Systems and trying to sell the hoard himself,"

Davy explained.

"Well, that cheeky bastard!" Michael said.

"Philbeen 9, eh?" Jake said. "Good. That'll buy us some time. Keep helping me get this thing space-born."

Jake went to the middle of the ship's long connecting corridor from the cargo section to the crew and flight deck. He performed the actions that Davy instructed. Turning, he moved further toward the cockpit.

At the interconnecting airlock, he pressed the button to open—another hall, then another airlock to the flight compartment. The door opened.

"Ah!" Jake shouted. "I just nearly shat me-self!"

"What happened?" Michael asked as he came down the hallway. He too stopped and stared.

In the pilot seat was an old-time vac suite. Jake approached cautiously and peered around the helmet.

"It was once a person… I think…" Jake began. He read the cloth patch with the name on the breast of the suit. "Commander Lake."

"What!" Michael said. "If this is Lake, then who in the name of the nayforic blitz spread the rumor of his treasure?"

"The atmosphere gage on the suit reads it was flooded with carbon dioxide. Looks like he was murdered – maybe," Jake said. "No time to figure that out." He unbuckled the corpse and tossed it into the hall. He sat down. "Davy, take me through the sequence to get these engines hot."

Davy triggered the hanger doors. As they opened, dust rained down on the transparent cockpit. Jake throttled up the VTOL thrusters, and the craft came off the deck. It took little energy in the low gravity to hover. He increased the power – the ship slipped up and out, rising into the dark expanse of vacuum.

"Davy, what are these extra switches for?" Jake asked.

"They're not on the schematic," Davy replied. "Perhaps they have something to do with those odd bits and pieces connected to Solomon's ship?"

"Don't mess with them," Michael said.

Jake throttled up, and the ship attained forward momentum. In his ocular-visor, he saw a holographic representation of the immediate asteroids.

"Track out," Jake said. In his vision, he now had a map of the wider sector.

"These are the mappings that Solomon made," Davy stated. "They may not be completely accurate anymore."

"So, you've already jumped?" Jake asked.

"We've folded and are traveling the closest path to Philbeen 9. I don't think that Solomon's craft's space-time displacement engine will get you there in one shot."

"Shit! Okay – I don't need the negative vibes, Davy."

Jake looked at the set of three buttons on the cockpit dash and shrugged his shoulders. "What the hell…" He pressed the blue button furthest on the right.

Immediately, Jake knew he'd made a mistake. The cockpit flared in bright amber light. He heard Michael cry out but then was surrounded by silence. Inside, he felt like all his nanobots were clawing at his bones and muscles to get out. There was a whooshing sound in his ear.

"Jake, I've picked up that you've become a singularity…" Davy's voice was distant, as if in the furthest reaches of a vast tunnel. "What do you see?"

In Jake's vision, he saw ever-expanding lines like a spiderweb – glistening in liquid silver, stretching out to infinity. His mind was desperately trying to comprehend what was happening. "Web…" was all Jake could manage.

"Your quantum implants are surging. In fact, they're gaining q-bits…" Davy said, surprised. "This is highly improbable."

Jake was envisioning his ship and Davy. In that

space of his imagination, a host of equations and numbers burst into existence as a brilliant red light, then faded. A small pulse of color appeared along a retreating thread of the web.

"I see you," Jake clumsily said.

"You see me?" Davy asked.

"Yes, the Bailiwick." Jake's voice carried sudden confidence, and he imagined Philbeen 9. "There."

Solomon's ship faded into reality, and Jake's eyesight came into immediate clarity. Alarms blared inside the cockpit. Closing on them was another vessel, which course-corrected in time to miss them.

"Unidentified ship – you nearly collided with us! Have your advanced navigation controls checked at the first shipyard!" an angry voice squawked at Jake.

Jake's muscles were locked, then he had movement again. Reaching for the controls, he noticed in his ocular-visor the spiderweb was gone, and now he saw a traditional view of his pilot controls. He looked over at Michael in the co-pilot chair.

Michael was drooling and babbling. His eyes were wide with terror and confusion.

"We're four hundred thousand klicks from Philbeen 9," Jake said. "Michael, get your hamper in order!"

"Jake," Davy began. "I'm not sure how to tell you this, but you moved independently to time-space."

Jake took a moment. "What the nog do you mean? We teleported?"

"Indeed, you did." Davy's voice was filled with both shock and curiosity.

"I remember plotting a course to Philbeen 9," Jake said. "That took some time."

"To you, it took time. But for you to travel, and reform into the original mass that you started with, that took no time at all," Davy told Jake.

"Not possible," Michael said.

"It seems very possible – considering you did it," Davy replied.

Jake looked over his shoulder at the corpse of Solomon Lake. "So, the ship really didn't need to move at all. We could have stayed in the hanger, started the teleporter device, and ended up here?"

"Quite possibly," Davy said. "I'm not sure how the navigation works with that device."

"What's your estimated time of arrival?" Jake asked.

"Three hours and fifty-two seconds," Davy said. "It does take time to compress through a sixth dimension from all the way over at the spiral arm."

"Donald still doesn't suspect anything?" Jake asked.

"No. He's content, sitting on the bottom bunk talking with prospective buyers of the cargo."

Jake found the controls for the ship identification beacon. "I guess we'd better figure out what this craft is called." The display showed all vital legal details – where the ship was purchased, how much it cost, the title owner, the naming location, and the name. "Ah, here it is... The Silver Horn. Damn... this ship is six hundred years old. It's an antique."

"An antique with a teleport drive connected to it. We can't let this fall into the wrong hands," Michael said.

"I agree. Our hands are as far wrong as it should fall," Jake retorted. "Since we have some time, let's link up to the local orbiting rest-stop. I have it on scopes now. Plotting a conventional course now at a thousand meters a second."

Michael got up and wandered back to where the corpse was. He knelt and then looked over at Jake. "He's been gnawed upon."

"What?" Jake's voice contained a hint of alarm.

"De-fleshed along the side of his skull and down

one side. No damage to his helmet. No weapon I know of could have done that," Michael said. "Highly unlikely it was self-inflicted. The gage shows the suit is filled with carbon dioxide and no oxygen."

"That's quite odd," Jake said as he began to reduce the ship's speed. He called up the STC and got a landing pad. As he settled down on the landing zone, the young STC controller spoke.

"That ship – The Silver Horn, keeps coming up as being missing or stolen. There's no modern ship with that name. In fact, it seems to have belonged to… Solomon Lake!"

"Yup – and he's with us and still the captain," Jake said.

"What?" the young man asked, sure that he didn't hear the reply correctly.

"Solomon Lake – he's here with me," Jake confirmed. He cut the engines and dropped the power to standby. Switching the comm to just Michael, he added, "Come on, let's make a shit-storm for our friend Donald."

Chapter 8
The Gentler Gamester

The Silver Horn connected its docking tube with the privately-owned Safe-harbor Rest Platform. Once the docking airlock showed positive pressure between the retractable causeway, Jake cycled the inner hatch open and stepped into the corridor. Michael followed.

As Jake rounded the last corner and exited into the lobby, he was met with a cacophony of shouts and questions from the gathered media.

"Sir, where did you find Solomon Lake's ship?" yelled one reporter.

"Someone said Solomon Lake is with you – where is he?" another shouted.

"Do you plan to sell it to a museum?" called another.

A young woman with a drone-cam pushed through the crowd. "Was there any treasure in the ship or where you found it?"

Jake cleared his throat. "I'll give a briefing after we've had some rest. Meet me here in the lobby at 1600 hours station-time. Until then – no comment." Jake and Michael headed toward the traveler's hotel.

"1600 hours is just two hours from now," Michael said.

"And, about 50 minutes from when Donald will be arriving with my ship. We have some knavery to perform in the meantime," Jake told Michael.

Michael smiled a cagy grin.

As soon as Jake was inside his room, he connected to the inner-communication link via the Reach-out Service. He set up a closed-link crypto-bank account and added ten thousand credits to it. Then, he made a call to a friend with a murky reputation.

At 1600 hours, Jake and Michael were back in the

lobby. The swarm of reporters was twice as thick this time.

Using his nonverbal comm, Jake reached out to Davy. "You still on track to drop out at Philbeen 9 in 53 minutes?"

"We are indeed, Jake," Davy said.

"Send me the drop-in coordinates and make sure that you back up all the ship's data once you get here. There's going to be a bit of nastiness when you arrive," Jake said, then turned to the gathered crowd. "My name is Jake Sharkar, and this is Michael O'Tool. We discovered the Solomon Lake ship and treasure a few days ago after an exhaustive search. Our colleague, Donald Newt, will be arriving shortly with the full allotment of the treasure in our hold. Once he arrives, he will be more than willing to discuss this extraordinary discovery with any who want to interview him." Jake gave a quick wink to Michael. "I'm providing the entry coordinates to you all, so at least a few of you can be the first to get his impressions of our efforts and journey."

"Michael raised his hands – the reporters quieted down. "Until Mister Newt arrives, we will reserve our statements. Until then, Jake and I will be in the hotel bar."

Both Jake and Michael began walking down toward the hotel and the bar – followed closely by shouting reporters and their drone-cams.

Jake checked his shipboard time – forty minutes to go until Donald folded into their sector. Davy provided updates every five minutes. At that exact point, Jake thought, Donald will find a crowded landing point filled with media, the local militia, looky-loos, and a contingent of the nearby Host System Navy.

Michael took a drink from his glowing Pilsy-push cocktail then sat back. "You have a giddy air about you, Jake," he said.

"Improvisation is the mother of all screwups – but sometimes, those powers that govern the universe take pity on we fools," Jake replied.

"Thirty-five minutes your time, Jake," Davy said.

Standing, Jake looked down at Michael. "It's time."

"If it must be – then better to have the crust of a sandwich than no sandwich at all," Michael replied.

"Millicent?" Jake spoke into his comm.

"Ready and waiting, Jake. This payout had better be worth the risk," Millicent said.

"Just don't do anything to tip your hand until we're in the shit," Jake said. He switched comm links. "Davy – you're still okay with what we need to do?"

"Jake – I was always considered a temp. If you can save any of my metadata, that would be appreciated, though."

"Jake, the Raiders are asking for an update," Michael said.

"Tell them to stay by the Whisky 687 sling-station. When I give the word – unleash hell," Jake replied.

"Thirty minutes, Jake," Davy said.

Jake reached down and lifted his half-empty glass of scotch. He drank it down and set the glass on the table. "Okay – pass the word. All is go!"

"Twenty Minutes, Jake," Davy announced.

"Davy – prepare to do your thing. And – may the universe have pity on our idiot endeavors!" Jake stated as he began walking toward the landing facility and the Silver Horn.

* * *

"Davy – once we pop, do a deep scan of the sector. I'm expecting a Ferret Freighter with plenty of cred-transfer ability," Donald said.

"As you wish, captain," Davy said. "We are five minutes to emergence. You may want to prepare for window-clarity."

Donald sat back in the navigator seat and put his

feet up on the control panel. He pulled out a zip-stick and inhaled the musky and powerful stimulant. "You know, that Jake had a pretty nice ship – even if it was old."

The ship shuddered - the windows cleared. All around were ships – hundreds of ships at his location. Camera drones were everywhere.

"Donald Newt, this is Davey Phelps of Galactic News Channel sixty thousand. What amazing discoveries have you brought the galaxy?"

Donald sat up, choking on the vapor he'd just ingested. "Who --" he got out before the ship lurched and trembled. "Davy, what the fuck!"

"We're under attack. I can't maneuver because of the many other ships in our vicinity," Davy said. There was a shudder again. "The exterior has been breached at the aft. There is a boarding party in the ship."

"Are they Host System Marines?" Donald asked.

"Negative – they…they are a sky-biker gang called the Raiders. They're moving toward the cockpit. I can delay them, but they have breaching tools," Davy stated. "I'll have the escape capsule ready upon your entry."

Donald pulled from his suit his pistol. "They're not taking this cargo!"

"I forgot to tell you that Pork Belly is leading the Raiders. They're armed with gauze weapons. I'd be concerned what they'd do to your paralyzed body once they have you," Davy said.

"Donald stood for a moment, then said, "Nogging shit-scarpers! Okay, I'll blast out of here!" He made his way to the side of the cockpit, pressed the command panel, and the door to the escape pod opened. He looked back into the cockpit. "Davy, set destruct five minutes." He closed the hatch and hit the large red button to jettison. There was a mighty blast – he was pressed into the crash-pads, then the pod was away careening toward Philbeen 9.

Jake set his feet on the deck of his old ship. Millicent was there. She rushed in and quickly opened a side panel. Jamming in some components, she moved her hands around in midair as she configured some powerful q-code.

The lights went out, then they came back up. The Raiders were looking around – at a loss for what to do.

Michael was standing at the rear cargo hatch. "The escape-pod light is blinking," he said.

"Donald must have jetted out." Jake examined some control data. "The pod is gone, and there is no one in the cockpit."

"Hey, Jake – we didn't get to kill no one!" Pork Belly declared with an almost emotional tone.

"No worries, fellas," Jake said. "The creds are in your crypto-account at the clubhouse. Check it – it's golden!"

"So, we're not going to get to clip no one?" Pork Belly asked.

"Not this trip. You guys did a splendid job, no killing needed at this point," Jake replied.

The Raiders came filtering back. Pork Belly barely fit between the cargo containers and the wall. In his hand was a breach-bar 600, and in the other hand, a 20-gage hand pistol. He eyed Jake with those far off dead eyes.

"How 'bout I kill this skiffer here?" Pork Belly pointed at Michael – who looked nervous.

"I heard that the Venoms made a public statement that the Raiders drink like pie-hole dandies," Jake said.

Pork Belly came over to Jake and gripped his vac suite by the chest-flap. He lifted Jake and looked deeply into his helmet. "Who the nog said this?"

"Billy Boy Boggs," Jake said.

"Fucking Billy Boy!" Pork Belly shouted. "He has a kill'en coming – come on fellas!"

The Raiders filed out and quickly EV'd over to several small – stolen – ships. In one minute, they were gone.

From all around, the media ships and bystanders were beating a fast exit fearing further fighting and possible damage to their own vessels.

"The destruct is off, and the new Davy is installed. You're back in command," Millicent called out.

Jake rushed up to the cockpit. "Davy, what's the situation?"

"A Host Systems destroyer coming in. They're demanding that all the media ships clear off. Now's our chance!"

"Take us out with the trash," Jake said.

Millicent crammed an obfuscating chip into the obfuscator. "This will work on them for a short time – my own special recipe. I'd suggest that we sweep by the Whisky 687 sling station and pick up the Silver Horn."

"Davy – take us to the Silver Horn," Jake ordered.

They tacked at the same rate as the other ships trying to clear a hole for the naval destroyer and its escorts. The Bailiwick 286 sailed past the military contingent just like the others.

"Don't make it obvious, Davy, but start heading to Whisky 687. Make it look like that's where we always go when routed by a destroyer," Jake said.

"I'm on it," Davy said. "And Jake, I'm sorry that I was reprogrammed for evil and didn't tell you."

"Davy – you called me Jake!" Jake said.

"Millicent was able to infuse some of that meta-data into the new upload – from personality two."

"Glad to have you again in the muck with us."

"Just as always," Davy replied.

The Bailiwick faded further and further away toward Whisky 687. On the far side, the Silver Horn was docked. Michael came into the cockpit. "So, what's the plan from here?"

"Well, considering I was not sure that that plan would work, I'm at a loss." Jake shrugged. "Donald will figure out in short order that we grabbed the ship and cargo, but he won't be able to use the Host System resources to come after us. They know now that he attempted to steal our stolen booty from them."

"Try for the Draber System. I know someone who will be more than happy to help us," Millicent said.

"Who?" Jake asked.

"Sam 'the killer' Valicore," Millicent said.

"The killer?" Michael asked.

"More a description than a formal name," Millicent added.

"That's what I thought it was to begin with!" Michael stated.

"Okay, I'll take the Silver Horn, you and Millicent take the Bailiwick. Give me the location where we'll meet," Jake said. "Wait – I'm getting a message."

Jake opened the encrypted comm. "Jake – I don't know how the fuck you pulled this off – but I'm not going to let you claim a sovereign credit for that shit!" Donald said.

"Create and send encrypted," Jake commanded. "Hey, Donald – you lose, and I win. Live with it!" Jake smiled. "Include picture and send message."

Millicent sent Jake the navigation information. "Jake – don't be late. Sam's as shady as they come – so I'd like to keep an exit route that the planetary defenses won't know about."

Jake again smiled. "No worry, my rash darling – you can trust in old Jake. I have one helluva an ace in my sleeve."

Jake went down the corridor to the hatch of the Silver Horn. He cycled the airlock and went up to the wheelhouse - stepping over the corpse of Solomon Lake. Strapping himself into the pilot's chair, he disconnected from the causeway – used the starboard thrusters to push off from the station. He throttled up the engines and headed away from any strong gravity wells in the area.

Once in position, he pressed the blue button.

Chapter 9
A Stitch In Time

The nano-bots again went crazy in his body. There was pain, then confusion, then a sudden awareness that nearly overwhelmed Jake.

That vast quicksilver web was in every direction he was conscious of. There was nothing intuitive about what he was seeing – yet, he had a complete understanding of how it worked.

There were dips in the time-space fabric, places where some powerful energy pinched a ruffle of space. Black holes, quasars, neutron stars, massive red giants, tiny blue suns, binary stars, and habitable planetary systems… Jake knew where they all were throughout multiple galaxies.

He thought of the coordinates that Millicent sent him. "There you are," Jake said, and focused on a point outside the metropolis of Saint York, on the planet of Lipton Fare.

It was so easy – to think of where you wanted to be, and the location would present itself in his ocular-visor. He dropped his landing gear and shut down his engines. "There," he said aloud.

Jake's muscles were locked – his hands tightly gripping the controls. There were green trees all around, and yellow grass waving in a gentle breeze. He regained control over his muscles again. His heart was racing, and his pulse thumped at his temples.

The glistening teleportation navigation system was no longer in his ocular-visor. Slowly, he stood and made his way to the galley, where he ordered a stiff drink and a nutrition bar. He drank down the whiskey, then consumed the bar. Taking out a zip-stick, he inhaled a solid dose of the chemical. His mind cleared and all sense of anxiety faded.

Putting on his planet-side clothes, he cycled the airlock and exited the ship. The air was crisp and clean. The landscape was rural, though he knew he was in the middle of a vast city. Somewhere, not far, the rippling of a brook sounded.

Jake made his way toward the bubbling water. On the bank, he noted a wide-open field with picnickers sitting and enjoying the day. In the distance, he saw the many archologies rising miles into the sky.

"Davy – how long until you drop into this solar system?" Jake asked.

"Sixteen minutes," Davy said.

"I landed in Primary Park in a grove of trees. I'll hail a lifter to take me to Sam's bar and brothel," Jake said.

"See you there," Davy stated.

Jake ordered a lifter, and the autonomous craft landed in the clearing. Jake got in and listed the destination. He was off. A few minutes later, he was standing in front of a sign rapidly shifting in red-green-blue colors. He pulled out a zip-stick and inhaled.

Upon entering the club, he was hit with a powerful scanner. In front of him, a small widow went clear, and a service-bot spoke.

"Enter the next room. You have no weapons and are clear to party. Don't forget to set your cred-wallet to auto-charge, if you want uninterrupted playtime.".

Jake double-checked his setting – it was on 'prompt to pay'. He'd leave it that way.

The first thing that hit Jake as he entered the second room was a blast of Heaven-scent. His nose implants immediately filtered the vapor. He definitely did not need to be dopy for this meeting.

The room was dark, filled with small orange glowing balls of plasma over each round table. Music was playing, and a crowd of patrons milled about.

Sex-bots were moving about drumming up trade, while biologicals enjoyed food and drink in copious amounts. An attractive young lady approached Jake.

"Look – I need some slippery-tide, are you in or out?" she asked.

Jake smiled at the proposition for sex. "Normally I'd be in, but I'm meeting someone."

She turned around fast, hitting Jake in the face with her spinning iridescent blue hair. "Suit yourself!" She moved back into the room, through the crowd, and to the bar.

A service bot came over. "Can I fit you with a table?"

"Sure," Jake pointed to a corner across the dance floor. "That table over there."

"Good choice, sir," the bot said.

The broad-shouldered bot pushed its way through the crowd – a menu in its hand and wearing a smart-fitting tuxedo. At the table, it waited for Jake to sit, then it set down the menu.

"May I bring you a drink?"

"I'll have a simbian fizz," Jake said.

"Right away, sir," the bot stated, then headed across the darkened room.

It was places like this that Jake really liked – a sense of nostalgia – the ancient bar ambiance that lured in those seeking something more primitive and packed with character.

The bot returned and set the crystal goblet on the table. "We have all forms of food here," it said.

Jake perused the menu. The holo-pictures changed every few seconds, and he put his finger on the image of a savory, and crispy roast-beast filet.

"Excellent choice, sir. The simulated flesh is of the finest quality." The bot spun and was off again.

"Davy?" Jake commed.

"We've just landed and are having the ship secured for an extra cost," Davy said.

"What do you think? Ten minutes until you get to

Sam's Place?" Jake asked.

"Probably. Millicent and Michael still have to pass through customs."

"I'm at a table across the dancefloor."

"I'll let them know," Davy replied. "Jake…?"

"Ya?"

"I've discussed this with Millicent, and there is a very good possibility that I can be connected to the circuits of the Silver Horn. Would that be okay with you?"

"Sure – knock yourselves out," Jake said.

Pushing the plate away, Jake rubbed his belly. He hated it when he stuffed himself so much that he felt uncomfortable. He drank down a dark stout, all the while keeping an eye on the front entry. After forty minutes, Millicent came in, followed by Michael. She scanned the room, set eyes on Jake, then approached.

"Sorry we're so late. Had to do some stuff first." Millicent waved over the service bot. "Anyway, tell Sam that I'm here," she said. "And, bring me a millpur sandwich with extra fried fleepox, and a glass of red wine." She sat.

Michael sat across from both. He took a menu from the bot and ordered. A few minutes later, the meals arrived. Jake ordered a scotch and sat back.

A well-dressed older man approached. He had a round face with graying temples and a scar from his nose to his chin. His suit was synth-silk cut to fit.

"Millicent, darling," the man said.

Standing, Millicent leaned into the fellow and allowed him to kiss her on both cheeks.

"Please – keep enjoying your food and beverages. I'm Sam, and consider your meal complementary. She," he pointed to Millicent, "is such a dear love. So clever when making ships invisible to the authorities."

"Come now, Sam, don't need to butter both halves of the bread," Millicent said. "We all know why we're here. Do you want to make a deal, or shall we shop around?"

Sam regarded them all with eyes that stared into the abyss. "You are such a flirt," Sam said. "I've thought about it, and I'd like to make you an offer." He nodded to Millicent.

Millicent got the offer in her ocular-visor. She choked on her wine. "That's all you're offering?" Her voice was filled with acumen.

"Look – honey – you're looking for a fence, and a fence never pays more than he thinks he can sell an item for. I know you – and your friends - were hoping for some unprecedented payout, considering the items. But I'm just a simple businessman, not a nation-system."

"I think you need to ratchet that cred amount up a bit. Even as a fence, you must know you're low-balling us," Millicent said.

"Okay. How about this amount?" Sam nodded.

"Sammy – you sure know how to disappoint a woman," she quickly retorted. "Take it up some more."

Sam nodded again.

"Now – that's getting there. Add another zero on the end, and I'll feel confident in passing this to my partners," Millicent said.

Sam's eyes drifted from one person to the other at the table before his gaze returned to Millicent. "You are insufferable," he said and waved over the service bot. "See that they are given any fare on the house."

"Yes, sir!" the bot replied.

Millicent sent the figures over to Michael and Jake. Both men remained composed. Jake responded, and Millicent acknowledged. "Sammy – I think we have a consensus. We'll take your offer. Have it broken three ways and transferred to these encrypto-banks. Once the money is there, I'll hand over the goods."

"Now hold up, little lady," Sam said. "Until I inspect the goods, there will no transfer of creds to anywhere."

The service bot brought Sam a tumbler of orange liquid. "We'll exchange off-world. Here are the coords." He nodded to Millicent. "Once I've had the stuff authenticated, then I'll take all that you got, and send the creds to wherever you want."

"Okay, Sammy…We'll be there. See you in six hours."

Sam smiled in an unnerving way, sipped his drink, turned, and left.

"He's going to try and nog us in the trouper, isn't he?" Michael said.

"Maybe," Millicent casually stated. "We'll need to be cleverer than they."

Jake finished his scotch. He took out a zip-stick and inhaled deeply.

"They don't call him 'the killer' for nothing."

Millicent and Michael took the Bailiwick up. It didn't take long for them to reach the rendezvous point.

Jake used the teleport switch. The Silver Horn popped onto an asteroid not far from the meeting point. Pain from the teleport process made his joints ache, and his muscles cramp. Once his muscles were back in his control, he reached out to Millicent.

"I'm in position," Jake said.

"We already have a ping from Sam's ship," Millicent responded. "Don't let us get murdered, old friend."

Davy commed in. "Jake – I've been connected up with the enviro-management system on the Silver Horn, and I have something disturbing to tell you about the corpse of Solomon Lake."

"What is it?" Jake asked.

After Davy explained, Jake asked, "You mean we've been flying around with that on the ship?"

"I do indeed," Davy said.

"Okay – thanks for telling me. That explains why Lake's suit was flooded with CO_2. He must have been trying to stop them from eating him. We'll sweep 'em out at the next opportunity – wait, I have an idea--"

"Jake, I don't think you understand. They're dormant – not dead," Davy interrupted.

"Don't worry, lad, I do understand. And, that will work just fine for me." Jake commed Millicent. "What's happening there?"

"They're on their way over now," Millicent said.

Jake waited. He waited and waited and waited some more. "Davy, what the nog is going on there?"

"You'll need to talk to Sam 'the killer'," Davy said. "He's insisting that you call him. I'm going to call this a bad situation."

Jake ground his teeth. "Okay." He commed off with Davy and rang Sam.

"Ah – there you are," Sam greeted. "I was going to put your friend Michael out the airlock when he started babbling about a corpse you have on your ship. The corpse of Solomon Lake?"

"You are a skeevy sot," Jake said. "I'll trade the corpse for Michael and Millicent."

"Fair enough," Sam replied. "Bring me the body, and I'll grant you three safe conduct out of the system."

I'll be along shortly," Jake snapped.

Jake ramped up the thrusters and angled the ship toward the navigational points of the Bailiwick and Sam's ship. They were a hundred thousand kilometers away. It would take him a few minutes to get there by normal means.

"Davy…"

"Yes, Jake?

"Sam's thugs – where are they?"

"They're in support positions around the ship," Davy responded. "Two are on the flight deck, two in the cargo hold, and two in the airlock. There are also four milling about in the galley."

"He brought ten with him? Any in the toilet?"

"Nary a one."

"Nary?" Jake quipped. "And the toilet can be environmentally sealed, right?"

"Of course," Davy said.

"Can you isolate the airflow and the scrubbers so they are in a close-loop into and out of the toilet?" Jake asked.

"Of course."

"Then do so on my command. After that, I want you to go on full comm lockdown for a count of forty minutes."

"Aye-aye," Davy confirmed.

"Good. Then, I think we have a really good chance at getting out of this pickle," Jake said.

"I always thought that was an odd expression," Davy replied.

Jake brought the Silver Horn alongside the Bailiwick and Sam's large junk-harvester ship. He matched the rotation of the two ships and did a soft-dock. He cycled the airlock and was met by Sam and Donald.

Chapter 10
The Flea in the Ointment

Donald chuckled. "Surprised to see me?"

"Donald has graciously – with the full backing of the Host Systems – agreed to take this alien junk off my hands at a considerable price. Thrown in for an extra fee, I'm handing over you three." Sam nodded to Millicent and Michael. "Donald here will take us over to Station 28D, where authorities are waiting."

"So – Jake, I just couldn't live with it," Donald jibed.

"Go fetch my Solomon Lake mummy," Sam said. Two thugs moved past Jake and came back with the corpse of Solomon Lake from the Silver Horn.

"Now, how did you beat me here, Jake?" Donald asked.

"Why should I tell you?" Jake retorted.

"Because if you don't, Michael will go out the airlock," Donald said.

"Okay. The Silver Horn – it has an alien teleport engine connected to the ship. I hid the control in the vac suit of Solomon," Jake admitted.

The greed in Sam's eyes was almost glowing. "Teleportation? And it works? That changes things, Donald my friend. I want another billion for the lot."

Donald looked annoyed. "I can't agree to that unless I communicate with my boss. But, I suspect they'll agree – for a working teleporter."

"Good – make sure it happens," Sam warned Donald. "If you don't mind, fetch me that control," Sam said to Jake.

"Wait – don't trust him," Donald said.

"I get that a lot," Jake told Sam as he moved toward Solomon's mummy.

"Wait!" Sam commanded. "He might have a

projectile pistol hidden in there. Monroe – you check the corps for the control."

A muscled fellow came over and unzipped the suit, then rummaged around inside. He pulled out a small comm bracelet – like those worn six hundred years earlier.

"Nothing in here but this, and some dust," Monroe said as he brushed off the dark material.

Jake edged his way toward the toilet door while everyone was gawking at Solomon and Monroe. Millicent and Michael did the same. In one motion, Jake leapt into the bathroom and pulled Michael and Millicent in with him. He shut the door.

"Davy, now!" Jake said.

"Your command is my wish," Davy replied.

There was a pounding on the door.

"Jake! Millicent! You three can't hide in there forever. Your little ruse didn't let you escape. You got in the crapper and not the escape pod!" Sam's voice called from the other side.

"We didn't want to leave," Jake responded.

"We're going to fly to the station, and the Marines will cut you out of that toilet," Donald told them.

"I don't think so!" Jake called back.

"You're being an idiot. Fine – stay in there," Donald said.

From the other side of the door, Jake heard Sam ask one of his men why he was scratching. The response was, he had a sudden rash.

A few minutes went by as they heard someone planning to head over to the Silver Horn and detach it from the soft-seal.

"That rash is getting really bad," someone said.

"What's that flashing light above the airlock?" another voice asked.

"That's the environment contamination warning light," Donald said.

Then – there came a panicked voice. "My skin is

crawling!"

"No – no – no!" Donald cried out. He started banging on the toilet door. "Open up and let me in!"

"Sorry, Don – but we're all filled up," Jake replied. "Should have just lived with it – like I suggested."

Screams of panic and cries of horror erupted. Jake looked over at Michael and Millicent. Both were under considerable strain as the screaming grew in intensity on the other side of the door. There were demands to open the door, then curses, then begging. But, Jake knew better than to open that seal.

"What the hell's going on, Jake?" demanded Millicent.

"Just clearing out some unwanted trash," Jake said.

"Whatever it is, it's not good," Michael whispered.

They waited in silence. When the forty minutes were up, Jake got a blip on his ocular-visor.

"Davy?" Jake asked.

"I'm here," Davy replied.

"How are the meat-fleas doing?" Jake questioned.

"Meat-fleas?" Millicent's voice was shaken.

"They've consumed all the biologicals in the ship, except you three," Davy informed Jake.

"Okay, vent the ship to vacuum, and let me know when all the fleas are washed out," Jake ordered.

"Will do, skipper," Davy said. "I'll use the drones to do some sweeping. Should be done in twenty minutes."

Jake went out first. He got into a vac suit and made sure that the body of Solomon Lake was secured in an air-tight container. After, Jake made sure that the whole ship was scanned twice for any unfriendly bio-signs. The vessel was declared clean.

"I wish that son-of-a-bitch Sam was still alive. I'd kick his dollops up between his teeth," Millicent snarled. "I still can't believe he'd double-cross me like that."

"No wonder Solomon didn't exploit his treasure," Michael added. "But who spread the rumor about his treasure? Who got the memory cubes out and into my hands?"

"Not to mention he contracted meat-fleas on one of his trips and died in his vac suit as a result," Jake said. "Thank the all-mighty programmer of the universe that those little bastards can remain dormant for so long." He looked around. "Now what?"

"I was about to ask you the same," Millicent said.

Both Jake and Millicent looked over at Michael. "Don't ask me. I'm just along for the money."

"Any other greedy shits you know who'd like to buy some alien tech?" Jake asked Millicent.

She shrugged and smiled. "Perhaps."

"Do you think you can figure out how to connect up that alien stuff into my ship?"

"Jake – for you – anything," Millicent said.

"Then let's get the nog out of here, and back to a safe haven," Jake suggested.

"Okay – you fly the Bailiwick, and I'll take the Silver Horn," Millicent said.

Jake couldn't hide his concern. "The process is a bit dangerous. I mean, there are unexpected effects of using that teleportation process."

She looked Jake in the eye. "Jake, old pal – every day is dangerous. And, I have to learn what I can about that stuff over there, if you want that I should implant it into your ship."

Jake couldn't argue with her logic. "Okay, but if you need help, I'll authorize you to use Davy. He is a great resource."

"Trumbelt 560," Michael suddenly said. "I know a guy who can get us a meeting with the Velmar Consortium. Those wanky-lanky fops have plenty of wealth, and I'm sure have a fetish for exo-art."

Jake chuckled. "Why not? I've already almost been

killed on this trip so many times I've lost count. Let's unload this crap and get back to just living."

Millicent sat in the pilot chair of the Silver Horn. She took the craft out beyond the major gravity well of the system.

"Alright, Davy, keep me in check," she said.

"Will do my best, my lady."

"That's a bit creepy – to call me your lady."

"I'll keep that in mind," Davy replied.

"let's take her out. Davy, I'm pressing the blue button," Millicent said.

"This won't be pleasant," Davy reminded her.

Millicent pressed the button, and all the nano-bots felt like they were clawing their way out of her muscles. She saw a vast quicksilver web in her ocular-visor.

"Now, your consciousness should be expanding – my lady," Davy said.

The pain in her limbs faded, and she became aware – aware that the universe was not infinite – that there were many verses out there, in every direction. In her vision, the web was like a Mandelbrot fractal – recursively falling away.

"Davy!" she cried out. "What is happening?"

"I've been waiting for you to connect," Davy said. "The expansion of your knowledge is growing. I am here for you."

"Davy?" Millicent said. "You're not Davy… who are you?"

"I'll tell you when you come to me, and we will discuss such things that will amaze even you," Davy said.

"Davy is just an AI. Who are you?" Millicent asked.

"I am the accumulated expansion of what you'd call alien technology – but I'm much more, so much more. Will you come to visit me?"

"I'll meet you," Millicent said. In her mind, there

was a flashing indicator among the shining web. She chose the location of the amber-colored blip and thought - go there.

* * *

Jake and Michael sat seaside on one of the golden-sand beaches of Udoria, the largest pleasure resort planet in the Host Systems planetary grouping of Kepler 890. Udoria did not have a close moon, so the vast oceans were an expanse of relative calm – often flat like glossy blue and green mirrors.

The temperature from the sun-baked the ground heating the air to 99 degrees – yearly average. Humidity along the coastal regions tended to remain at 80 – 90 percent, with occasional dramatic thunderstorms that illuminate the area with epic blasts of lightning.

Michael turned to Jake, who lay naked on a cloth and wood lounge chair. "So, still no word from Millicent?"

Jake reached over and took up his Thermo-cool glass of jipper-colada and consumed a long draw from the paper straw. "She's either absconded with the Silver Horn or been killed trying to fly that teleporting relic." He put down his drink and spread sunscreen on his limbs and chest.

"I'm going for a swim." Jake stood – his feet sinking into the soft golden sand.

"Don't let a water-titan snip off your dangler there," Michael laughed.

Jake shook his head with a slight chuckle. He walked past the many resort-courtiers and waded into the shimmering green waters up to his hips. He looked up into the dark blue of the sky and whispered,

"Millicent, old girl – where the nog are you?"

ABOUT THE AUTHOR

The author Lawrence BoarerPitchford has penned more than seven novels. He has created tales of fantasy often with dark overtones and flawed anti-heroes. Along with fantasy, he has written novels of historical fiction, and science fiction, all providing the reader with vivid settings and relatable characters sure to titillate the avid reader.

If you liked Jake and the Treasure of Solomon Lake, you may also like some of his other works. They can be found at Amazon Books.

Classic Fantasy

The Lantern of Dern Blackhammer
In the World of Hyboria
The Last Atlantian Prince

Steampunk/SciFi

Harrow's Gate
Jake and the Solomon Lake Treasure

Historical Fiction

Sawbones.
Thadius

Horror/ Mystery/ Detective

The Cox Head Horror